TRINITY ACADEMY

Cover Designer: Sybil Wilson, <u>PopKitty Design</u>

Cover Model: David

Photographer Credit: <u>Wander Book Club Photography</u>

TABLE OF CONTENTS

Dedication

Allyson, Sarah & Elaine.

Ladies, thank you for always encouraging me. I
appreciate everything you do for me!
I hope I'll get to write many books with you by my
side.

Songlist

The song Lake played for Lee

BTOB – <u>For You</u>

The music I listened to while writing

<u>Emotions</u>

Synopsis

His eyes have the power to undo all the hurt caused by
my family.

"Don't let them see you cry."

After months of refusing, I finally agree to move to
America, where my fiancé's waiting for me.
Just like my mother, an arranged marriage lies in my
near future.
Just like my mother, I'm probably going to be shoved
aside in a couple of years after providing the Cutler
family with an heir.

Being a Korean girl from a culture that's very different
from the west, it makes me stand out like a sore thumb.
There's nothing I can do but to accept the fate arranged
by my father and his mistress. My marriage to Lake
Cutler will be a business deal and nothing else.

My plan is simple. Make him hate me enough to break
off the engagement so I can return to Korea.
But I didn't account for those caring brown eyes.
What started as a mission to save myself from an
unhappy arranged marriage soon turns into a battle to
not lose my heart.

I dare him to walk away, but instead, he shows me any
bridge can be crossed.

Glossary

Abeoji - Father
Ajeossi - Sir
Andwae - It can't be/No way (Used for shock/fear/grief)
Aniyo - No
Annyeong - Hello (Informal)
Annyeonghaseyo - Hello/Morning/Afternoon/Evening (Formal)
Daebak - Cool.
Eomeo - Oh my (Surprised reaction)
Eomeoni - Mother (Formal)
Eomma - Mom (Informal)
Gwaenchanh-a - Are you okay?
Gwiyeobda - So Cute
Jeongmal gomapsseumnida - Thank you very much (Formal)
Joesonghamnida - I'm sorry (Formal)
Mannaseo pangapseumnida - Nice to meet you
Michin Nyeon - Crazy Bitch!
Ne - Yes
Salanghaeyo - I love you
U-wa - Wow!
Wea? - Why?
Ya - Hey!
Yeoboseyo - Hello (Answering a phone)

Gimbap: Korean-style maki sushi.
Kimchi: Spicy cabbage.
Mandu: Steamed dumplings.
Pajeon: Deep-fried pancakes.
Tteokbokki: Rice cakes in spicy sauce.

*In Korean culture, respect for age and status are very important, with hierarchy affecting all aspects of social interactions. Everyone has a role in society as a result of hierarchy - therefore it is vital to respect it. Status is largely determined by someone's role in an organisation, which organisation they work for, which university they went to, and their marital status.

Korean family names are mostly one syllable, while given names tend to have two. The family name comes first (Park Lee-ann). Until you are on very good terms with a Korean counterpart, it is best to use the family name preceded by an honorific (such as Mr), whether speaking directly to them or about them to another Korean. In settings that call for great respect or formality, you should use your counterpart's formal title and surname (Chairman Park). Some also view their name as a very personal thing, so a suggestion to work on a first-name basis may be slow to be offered.

Source Credit: ASIALINK BUSINESS

Prologue

Read Falcon & Mason before continuing with Lake as they are all interconnected.
While trying to stay true to Korean culture, some traditions may get lost in translation. Please see Glossary for explanations of terms and culture.

Lee

(Sixteen years old.)

Placing the beverage on the counter, I say, "Enjoy!" Then my eyes dart to the next customer. "Welcome. What would you like to order?"

After placing the order, Kim Min-young comes to stand next to me. "I'll take over."

"Thank you," I bow slightly, then walk to the back where the staff room is.

Taking my school uniform from my locker, I go to a cubicle and quickly take off my apron and work attire. I fold it before placing them neatly in a plastic sleeve. Pulling on my school clothes, I make sure everything is in its place, then I go to put the plastic bag in the locker and grab my backpack. Closing the locker, I hear my stomach rumble and patting it, I whisper, "Hold out a little longer. I'll eat when I get to the food stall."

Glancing at my watch, I make sure I have enough time to hand in my application for another part-time job before I have to go to Dongmun market so I can help Mom until we close at midnight.

I shrug on my backpack, and with a slight nod at the other employees, I call out, "Thank you for working hard. See you tomorrow."

Running out of the coffee shop, I almost bump into an elderly man. "I'm sorry, Sir," I quickly apologize with a bow while I keep running.

I make it to the restaurant on time, and stop to remove my application from my bag before I walk inside. I approach the first employee I see, "Where can I hand in my application for the dishwashing position?"

He points toward the back before he turns to welcome new customers.

I walk to where he gestured and stand on my toes, so I can see over a counter. There's a constant buzz of clattering pans, clanging pots, and sizzling heat. A chef walks by, and I quickly ask, "Where can I hand in my application for the dishwashing position?"

He shoots me a glare before he yells at one of the waiters who just dropped a plate of food.

Walking to my left, I peek down a hallway before I walk down it. Seeing an office to my left, I knock on the door and bow to the man behind the desk. "Where can I hand in my application for the dishwashing position?"

"Leave it there," he grumbles, pointing to the corner of the desk.

I bow again and quickly dart into the office. With both hands, I place the application where he indicated and bow again as I move backward. "Thank you."

When I'm out of the office, I jog down the hallway and dart to the side when a waiter comes out of the kitchen, carrying a tray of food. I wait for him to walk first, and when he turns left to walk to a table, I rush out of the restaurant and run as fast as I can.

I make it in time for the bus, which goes to Dongmun market, and climbing up the steps, I swipe my card and sit down in the first empty seat. Shrugging off my backpack, I hold it on my lap as I rest my forehead against the window. I have ten minutes to rest and letting out a sigh, I close my eyes. Seconds later they pop open when my phone begins to ring.

I quickly dig it out of the front of my bag and answer, "Hello?"

"Park Lee-ann, come home," Mom says, sounding short as aways because she hates talking over a phone.

"Why? Are you feeling sick again? I can still go manage our food stall on my own."

"No, come home. I closed the stall. Don't take long."

I let out a sigh, thinking about the money we're going to lose because we're not open tonight. "Yes, Mom."

I put the phone back in my bag and getting up, I press the button for the bus to stop. I move to the door and hold onto the pole, and when the doors open, I quickly step off the bus.

I shrug on my bag as I begin to jog in the direction of my neighborhood. Mom struggles with asthma, and working with the burners all day long isn't good for her health. If I can get a part-time job at the restaurant, then Mom won't have to work so hard. With the two jobs,

I'll have then, I will be able to make enough for our rent and food.

When I reach our neighborhood, I weave through narrow alleyways and dart up painted stairs. Nearing my home, I notice two men dressed in suits standing out front. As I turn up the short path and head to the steps leading up to the rooftop where our room is, I nod slightly. When they ignore me, I pull a face, and mumble, "Rude rich people."

I let out a tired breath when I get to the top and kick off my shoes before I open the door and walk inside. "Mom, I'm home. Why did –"

My eyes widen when I see a man sitting across from Mom by the table in our small room. Mom climbs up from her knees and gestures with both hands to the man, "This is your father."

I frown and pull my backpack off, but bow low, before I ask, "My father?"

"Come sit, Park Lee-ann," he barks.

My eyes dart to Mom, but she's already sinking down to her knees. I walk closer and kneeling, I place my hands on my legs and glance at my mom.

"You will be eighteen in two years," the man says. "I have arranged a marriage for you with an American man."

"What?" The word explodes from me. It takes a moment for my tired mind to catch up with what the man said. I turn to my mom. "What is this?"

Her shoulders slump. "Chairman Park Je-ha is your father. He allowed me to raise you. You need to listen to your father."

I shake my head and climb back to my feet. Pointing at Chairman Park, I say, "I don't know this man. How can you tell me to listen to him?"

"Please forgive her behavior, Chairman Park," Mom says hurriedly, bowing her head even more.

"Mom!" I cry as a desperate feeling crawls into my heart. Grappling for reasons why this is happening, I kneel back down and grab Mom's arm. "Is this about money? I applied for another job. If I get it, you won't have to work anymore."

She shrugs my hands off and gives me a strict glare. "Your place isn't with me any longer." Even though her face is set in hard lines, I don't miss the heartache in her eyes.

16

"You don't mean that," I whisper. My heart begins to pound in my chest as worry and fear swirl inside of me.

"You have to go with the Chairman," she says, sounding so very exhausted.

I shake my head and fight to keep the rampant emotions from swallowing me whole. "You don't mean that," I repeat. "He's a stranger. You won't let me go with him."

"He's your father."

I want to fall to the floor and cry until I can drown myself in my own tears, but pride keeps me from giving in to the emotion.

"If you swear to marry the man of my choosing, I will leave you with your mother until you are eighteen," the Chairman says.

That will give me two years to find a way to save both Mom and myself.

"I will also allow you to move into one of my buildings, so you don't have to live in this..." disgust ripples over his face as he looks at our precious few belongings, "room."

"We don't –"

Mom slaps the back of my head. "Forgive her Chairman Park. She's still young. We will be grateful for the two years."

His eyes settle hard on Mom, his mouth pulling down at the corners. "My secretary will be in touch. Park Lee-ann will have to be groomed, so she doesn't bring shame to my name."

"Yes, Chairman," Mom obediently answers.

I always thought my biggest problem would be making sure Mom and I don't starve. But as I watch the man stand up, and his cold eyes glare down at me, I realize dying should've been the least of my fears.

———————————

(Eighteen years old)
Sitting on the floor in my bedroom, I stare at the only photo I have of Mom.

I last saw her on my eighteenth birthday. It's been almost three months, and I'm only allowed to call her twice a week after I've spoken with Mr. Cutler without doing anything to shame the Chairman.

After the Chairman came to see us the first time, Mom told me she was married to him, but he got a mistress, and Mom divorced him. Because I wasn't a son, he let me go with her until he needed me.

The Chairman said he gave Mom enough money so she won't have to work anymore, for which I'm grateful because her health keeps deteriorating.

I tried to run away after the first week I was brought to the mansion, and my punishment for wanting to see Mom was to be locked up in this room.

I'm only allowed to interact with four people. The maid who brings me my meals. The tutor who provides my lessons on Western culture and the English language. Chairman Park's mistress, Jo Yoon-ha, who bore a son out of wedlock for the Chairman. And Mr. Cutler, my fiancé.

I hear the key turn in the door, and quickly get up from the floor. Placing both hands over my stomach, I lower my head as Jo Yoon-ha comes in with the phone.

"Read the messages I've exchanged with Mr. Cutler on your behalf. You have thirty minutes until you video call with him."

My eyes dart up. "Video call?"

19

She raises her hand so fast, I don't have time to duck before her palm connects with my cheek. The sting is fleeting, leaving a hot sensation in its wake.

"Read the messages and fix your face," she snaps and shoves the phone against my chest before she goes to sit in the chair by the window.

I unlock the screen, and my eyes scan over the words.

Mr. Cutler: Just four more days. Are you looking forward to coming here?

Park Lee-ann: Yes. I'm lucky to be marrying a handsome man like yourself.

Mr. Cutler: Besides going to the spa, shopping, and horse riding, what would you like to do when you get here?

Park Lee-ann: Anything that pleases you. I will do my best as your wife.

Mr. Cutler: Is there anything specific you would like to do or a place you would like to visit.

Park Lee-ann: I would like to spend time with your mother to learn what will be expected of me on our wedding night. I don't want to be a disappointment due to my inexperience.

Mr. Cutler: Don't worry about that. Let's first get to know each other better. I will call you tomorrow at 10am your time.

Park Lee-ann: Thank you for understanding. I look forward to talking to you.

I close my eyes as shame ripples over me. I don't get time to process it, because Jo Yoon-ha snaps, "Fix your face. Mr. Cutler will call in ten minutes."

"Yes, Ma'am," I whisper. I walk to the dressing table and sitting down, I struggle to lift my eyes to the mirror. Knowing I don't have time, I force my gaze up and reach for the powder. When my makeup looks perfect, my eyes lock with the reflection staring back at me.

I hate that you're pretty. I should cut off your hair and scar your cheeks so no man will look at you.

If I had my freedom, I would throw you into the Han river. I would rather die a thousand deaths than bear a child to a man who will discard me the same way my mother was discarded.

My arm is grabbed, and I'm yanked up. "You're so pathetic. To think Chairman Park's business deal depends on you is absurd. Unfortunately, the only way

Chairman Park can guarantee a return on his investment is for you to marry this man. Smile and don't bring shame to Chairman Park, or you will never speak to your mother again."

The phone begins to ring, and I force a smile to my mouth as I lift the phone up. I don't take in the face on the profile picture as I swipe up.

Mr. Cutler smiles when the call connects, and says, "Annyeonghaseyo, Park Lee-ann."

I stare at his face, taking in his brown eyes, his light brown hair, and the stubble on his jaw.

Jo Yoon-ha comes to stand in front of me, giving a dark glare filled with warning.

"Hello, Mr. Cutler. Thank you for calling me," the words fall automatically over my lips.

"Are you okay?" he asks, which has Jo Yoon-ha crossing her arms.

I force a wider smile around my mouth. "Yes, I'm fine. How are you?" My words are much slower than his, but at least my pronunciation is clear enough for him to understand.

"I'm good, especially now that I get to talk to you. Only three days, and then you're here."

Three days.

Three hopeless days. I'll just be transferred from one prison to another.

Because of the despairing feelings, I take too long to respond, and Jo Yoon-ha kicks my shin.

"I'm sorry," the words burst over my lips. "I was thinking of what it will be like there."

"Are you worried about anything?" he asks, and it makes me really focus on his face. That's twice he's picked up that I'm upset.

His eyes are focused on me, and when I meet his gaze, I feel apprehension slither down my spine.

This is a man. A foreign man. I haven't even kissed a boy yet. How will I deal with a man?

Jo Yoon-ha kicks me again, and I almost flinch but instead shift in the chair. "I'm just worried about the cultural differences," I admit a partial truth.

"Don't worry too much. I've been studying everything I could find about your culture. I don't expect you to change or to adopt my culture. We'll find a middle ground to make it work."

"Thank you."

"Lake, we need to... shit, sorry," I hear another man's voice.

"Sorry about that. I have to go, but I'll see you in three days." I nod, feeling relieved that the call is coming to an end. "Have a safe flight."

"Thank you."

The call ends, and Jo Yoon-ha grabs the phone from my hand before slapping the side of my head.

"You better learn how to act before we land in America, or I'll have your mother send to a place you'll never find her."

I want to jump up and lash out at her, but fear for my mother has me gripping the sides of the chair and keeping still.

"You should be happy. You get to marry a handsome, wealthy man instead of living in the slums with your mother."

When she leaves, locking the door behind her, I wrap my arms around myself. I miss my life before Chairman Park. Although I worked hard and had to do my homework at midnight, it was at least my own life.

Chapter 1

Lake

I take a seat at a table while I wait for the pizza order. Staring outside, my mind goes back to this afternoon.

I know Falcon and Mason are upset with the way things played out at the airfield, and believe me, I am too, but my hands are tied.

Until Mr. Park returns to South Korea, I have to be careful. Right now, he has all the power, but once he has invested and the marriage has been officiated, that will all change.

I've found out as much as I could about the Park family. From what I understand, Mr. Park is divorced from Lee's mother, and the woman he brought along on the business trip is his mistress who he has a son with.

Something has been niggling at the back of my mind, and the only thing I can contribute it to is that the tone of text messages from Lee just doesn't match the video calls I've had with her.

Maybe she's just shy talking face to face?

I shake my head and think back to our last video call. Her eyes kept darting up as if something was distracting her attention.

She could've been watching the time.

I let out a soft chuckle and murmur, "You're probably imagining things." I'm just on edge because of everything that's been happening with Layla and Kingsley.

I lean back in the chair and pull out my phone. Scrolling to Lee's number, I press dial and bring the phone to my ear.

When it goes to voicemail, I say, "Hey, Lee. I just wanted to hear if you and your family checked into the hotel okay. I'll see you tomorrow at the country club."

After I end the call, I cringe when I remember I forgot to speak to her with honorifics. I let out a sigh, and can only hope she won't be offended.

When my order is ready, I get up and collect it, then head out to the car.

Hey, at least I know there's nothing wrong with my car after Mason checked it out for me, and that the whistling sound I've been hearing was probably my imagination. Getting into Mason's car, I set the pizza boxes on the passenger seat. I pull on the safety belt, then start the engine before I drive back to the Academy.

A smile forms around my mouth when I think how beautiful Lee looked in person. Damn, I thought Kingsley was short, but even with heels on, Lee's head barely reached past my shoulder. She wore a simple black dress that flared from her hips, and her hair hung loose past her shoulders. Actually, beautiful doesn't begin to describe her.

I'll see her tomorrow at the country club, where our parents will sit down to discuss some of the terms for the deal and our marriage.

The deal. I grimace, really hating the word. There's no way I'll marry Lee if she doesn't agree to it one hundred percent. Honestly, it worries me whether she's being forced into this marriage, or whether she had a choice like I did.

As I near the campus, and indicate to turn left, a car comes speeding from the opposite side. While I wait for it to pass by, my phone starts to ring, and I glance at the screen before I answer. "What's up?"

"Kingsley's starving. Are you on your way back?" Mason asks.

"I'm right outside the gates."

"I'll come down so I can help you carry the pizzas," Mason offers.

"It's okay. I can –"

The approaching vehicle suddenly swerves in my direction and not thinking twice, I press hard on the gas, making Mason's Bugatti shoot forward as I turn the steering wheel sharply to the left.

The other car hits the rear end of the Bugatti, shifting me right off the road and onto the stretch of grass by the wall, near the front gate. My body slams against the side of the seat and door and a flash of panic has me looking through the back passenger window. In total shock, I watch as the other car flips before it crashes through the barrier only to disappear down the side of the mountain.

"Holy fuck!" My breathing begins to speed up, and my heart's hammering like crazy against my ribs.

"Lake!" I hear Mason's shout, but I'm too shocked to respond.

What the hell just happened?

My pulse races even faster as I unclip the safety belt, and getting out of the car, I run to the spot where the other car went over. Glancing down the mountainside, I can't see anything.

I quickly pull out my phone, but I'm shaking so much, I can't even dial 911.

"Lake!" I turn to the sound of Mason's voice and watch as he runs toward me with Falcon right behind him.

I hold my phone up and stupidly point down to where the other car must be. "The car just went over." My voice sounds distant, and I shake my head to get rid of the hazy feeling.

Falcon grabs hold of me, pulling me away from the edge where the barrier's been crashed through, then he keeps an arm around my shoulders.

With a look of disbelief, Mason asks, "A car went over?"

I nod and try to slow my breaths. "We need to call 911."

Security comes running out of the campus, which has Mason shouting, "What the fuck are you doing in that booth? I came from the dorms and still got here before you."

"We called for emergency services," the one guard explains, then he looks at me. "Are you okay, Mr. Cutler."

I nod but cover my mouth with a shaking hand while my eyes dart back to the broken barrier. "He didn't even brake. He just slammed into the rear of the Bugatti, flipped once, and then he went over," I whisper, shocked by what had happened in only a space of a couple of seconds.

Layla and Kingsley come running across the road, their eyes wide.

"I've never seen anyone run as fast as the two of you," Kingsley says breathlessly. "What happened?"

"A car went down the mountain," Falcon explains.

"What?" Layla exclaims.

"I need to call your mother," Mason says while pointing at Layla, then he takes my phone from me and dials a number. "Stephanie, there's been an accident right outside the front gate of the campus. A car hit my Bugatti, which Lake was driving before it went down the mountain. Get over here."

Falcon leans a little forward and catching my eyes, he asks, "Are you sure you're okay?"

I nod again. "Just shocked out of my mind."

"Lake," Kingsley comes to stand on my other side, placing a hand on my back, "don't you want to go sit down? You're shaking like a leaf in a shit storm."

I nod. "Sitting would be good."

Layla stays with Mason while Falcon and Kingsley walk me back to the Bugatti. When Falcon opens the passenger door, he cringes. "There's pizza everywhere." He shuts it and says, "I'll go get a chair from the security booth."

"Don't worry." Not caring where I sit right now, I lower myself to the grass, and lean back against the door.

The sound of sirens fills the air, and soon the area is covered with emergency services and police officers.

Someone crouches next to me, and when I glance up, I see Stephanie's worried face. "Lake, are you alright?"

I nod for what feels like the hundredth time. "Thank God," she whispers as she pulls me into a hug. "I think I just lost ten years of my life from worry."

I turn my head, so I can rest my cheek on her shoulder, but before I can close my eyes, a paramedic hurries toward us. I have to assure him a couple of times that I'm fine before he checks my vitals and recommends I see a doctor.

When I'm finally done answering questions and giving my statement, I get permission to leave the accident scene.

"I just heard a security guard tell one of the cops the driver was West Dayton," Kingsley whispers to Falcon.

"Which guard?" Falcon asks. I watch him walk to where Stephanie is talking with two cops and one of our guards.

Mason comes jogging toward me with Layla right behind him. "We can move the car," he says.

"Great," I reply and smile at Kingsley as she helps me to my feet. "I'm going to head inside then."

Before I can leave, Stephanie comes walking toward me. "Lake, I'll handle everything here. I'll call if I hear anything. Go rest."

"Was it really West Dayton?" I ask.

"As far as we can tell. The footage shows it's his car that went off the side, but until they reach the wreck, we can't be sure."

I glance at Mason, who doesn't show any expression on his face at hearing the news.

After the accident yesterday, I feel rattled. Falcon and Mason are like two mother hens, so I do my best to act like my normal self so they'll stop fussing.

Stephanie called late last night to let us know it was West who died in the accident. It sucks that he died so young, but damn, I can't exactly mourn his passing.

There's a knock on my door, and then Falcon pops his head into the room, "Are you ready?"

"Yeah, just need Mace to help with the tie," I say as I get up, but a wave of dizziness drags my butt back down to the bed.

"Lake?" Falcon rushes into the room and crouches in front of me. "Are you okay?"

"Just dizzy. They said it could take a while before I felt the effects of the whiplash."

"You sure it's just whiplash?" There's a worried frown on his face.

"I'm sure," I reply, and getting up again, I take it slower this time. "Mace, help me with the tie." I walk out into the living room and smile when I see Layla and Kingsley.

Kingsley lets out a low whistle. "Lee's ovaries are going to do backflips when she sees you."

"Thanks… I think," I let out a chuckle and turn to Mason. When he starts fixing the tie, Layla asks, "Why haven't you learned to make a tie?"

"It's easier to just let Mason do it." I grin her way, and when Mason pats me on the shoulders, I say, "Thanks, buddy."

Mason walks to Kingsley and presses a kiss to the top of her head. "I'll come by your suite when we get back."

Layla gets up to hug Falcon, and feeling like the odd one out, I walk to the table and grab my car keys.

"We're taking the Bentley, and I'm driving," Mason says before he gives Kingsley another kiss.

"Yes, Dad," I mumble, and dropping the keys, I walk to the door. Before I leave, I say, "Enjoy your freedom, girls."

"What freedom?" Mason grumbles while coming after me. Before he can wrap an arm around my shoulders, Falcon yells, "He's got whiplash! No chokeholds until he's better."

I turn and grin at Mason while we walk into the hallway. Not being able to resist the chance, I taunt, "No chokeholds until I'm better."

"Can I kick his ass? There's nothing wrong with the lower part of his body."

"Mason! Don't you dare bully Lake," Kingsley shouts.

"You're outnumbered." I begin to laugh, but it only makes a low throbbing start in the back of my head.

I close my eyes for a second, and it has Mason framing my face with his hands. "What's wrong?"

I push his hands away. "Just a headache."

Falcon comes out of the suite, and hearing my words, he asks, "Shouldn't we postpone the lunch for when you're better?"

"No, I'm fine. Let's get going before we're late."

When we walk out of the dorm, Falcon asks, "Are you sitting in the back?"

"Is that a trick question?" I grin. "It's a forty-minute drive. I'm sleeping all the way there." I unbutton my jacket and take it off before I climb into the backseat. Lying down, I close my eyes, willing the whiplash to not get worse.

When we reach the country club, and I wake from the nap, my neck feels even stiffer than before.

It's only for two hours. You can do this.

I get out of the car and pull on my jacket again. While I'm fastening the button, two more cars pull up. I watch the security get out of the first car, and then they open the back door, and Mr. Park steps out.

My eyes dart to the second car, and my eyebrow raises slightly when the mistress climbs out of the back, along with Lee.

"Please tell me I'm not the only one who thinks it's weird that they didn't drive together," Mason grumbles under his breath.

"Their culture is different from ours," I remind him before I turn to Mr. Park. I'm not sure whether I should bow or offer him my hand, but when his eyes just skim over me, I decide to do neither.

I watch him walk inside, and then Falcon asks, "Why didn't you offer to shake his hand?"

"He ignored me. He wouldn't have taken my hand, and I wasn't about to let him embarrass me."

Mason shakes his head. "Sorry, but this is all kinds of fucked-up. I don't like it one bit."

I glance at Mason. "Let's see how lunch goes."

"Mr. Cutler," I turn my head to the right, and it makes an unbelievable ache pulsate through my head.

Fuck, that hurts.

"Gwaenchanh-a?" the mistress asks if I'm okay, and luckily, it's one of the words I've learned, so I'm able to understand her.

"Yes, thank you," I answer, then I slowly turn to Falcon. "Take over."

I feel Falcon's hand on my back, and he quickly explains, "He's okay. He was in a car accident yesterday. You should go inside. We'll be right there."

I hear Lee translate Falcon's words, and then he says, "They've gone inside."

"I just turned my head too fast. You go ahead, I'll be there in a minute."

"I'll go. You stay with him," Mason orders, then he jogs into the country club.

"We should've postponed," Falcon mutters.

"Yeah, you're right. I just don't want to drag this thing out. Mr. Park comes across as an impatient man."

I take a minute, and fortunately, the ache subsides a bit, but my neck is still stiff as hell.

"Let's go in," I say as I begin to walk.

We head past reception, and as we're about to step into the dining area, someone bumps into me. I instinctively react and grab hold of the person.

"Eomeo!"

Glancing down, I'm met with Lee's wide eyes as she stands frozen with my hands on her arms. She slowly turns her head to where I'm touching her left arm, and it makes me quickly let go of her.

"Mr. Cutler, I'm sorry." She takes a couple of steps back and bows before she hurries past me.

"I don't think I'll ever get used to the Korean culture," Falcon mutters when we walk toward the table.

Chapter 2

Lee

My heart's racing in my chest as I rush to the restroom. When I lock myself in a cubicle, I lean back against the wall and take a couple of breaths.

This morning, Chairman Park told me he would be returning to Korea on Wednesday morning and that I would have to stay with the Americans.

I haven't had a moment alone to process any of it. Squatting down, I wrap my arms around my knees and bury my face in the fabric of the dress.

This can't be happening.

I don't want to be here. I want to go home.

I hear a door open, and then Jo Yoon-ha calls out, "Park Lee-ann, you're keeping your fiancé waiting!"

"Sorry," I call back and standing up, I flush the toilet before I step out of the cubicle.

She grabs my arm and yanks me to her. "Don't push me, or you'll never see your mother again."

"I'm sorry."

This woman has taught me how to hate. I will find a way to get back to Mom, and then I'll make Jo Yoon-ha pay.

When she lets go of the tight grip she has on my arm, I follow her out of the restroom. Bringing my right hand up, I rub the tender spot and glancing down, I grimace when I see the red finger marks above my elbow.

Chasing all emotion from my face, I take a seat next to Mr. Cutler. He slowly turns his head in my direction, and I lower my eyes to his hand, which is resting on his leg.

Will those hands be kind or cruel?

"Did I do that?" Mr. Cutler exclaims, sounding upset. My eyes dart up to his face, and then I sit frozen as he reaches for my arm. His touch is soft when he brushes his thumb over the handprint Jo Yoon-ha left on me.

"Shit, I..." He looks greatly disturbed by the thought that he has hurt me.

"No," I whisper. His eyes dart to mine, and tradition screams at me to lower my gaze, but there's something in his eyes that makes me stare.

"How did you get hurt?" he asks.

Would it change anything if I told you?

"Park Lee-ann," Jo Yoon-ha hisses under her breath.

I quickly lower my gaze. "I bumped into a wall," the lie spills over my lips.

His thumb brushes over the finger marks one more time, and then he murmurs, "I'm sorry you got hurt."

I nod and keep my eyes down as they begin to talk about business.

When the food is served, it's so bland and oily, I can only manage a few bites. I notice that Mr. Cutler doesn't touch his food either, and glancing at the Chairman and Jo Yoon-ha to make sure they're still listening to Chairman Reyes, I turn my head slightly to Mr. Cutler, and whisper, "Are you not feeling well?"

He turns his head too fast, and like earlier, his features tense with pain, but then the corner of his mouth lifts, and he smiles through whatever discomfort he's feeling. "I'm okay, thanks for asking." His eyes dart to Jo Yoon-ha, and he keeps looking at her when he asks, "Did she grab you?"

I quickly glance down at the mark that's luckily fading, but you can see it wasn't made by bumping into a door.

Not knowing what to answer, I just say, "I'm glad you're feeling okay."

"What is he saying?" Jo Yoon-ha suddenly asks, which has me slightly jerking with surprise.

"I asked if he's not feeling well. It looks like he's in pain."

"Good. Give him attention."

I try to smile as I look back at Mr. Cutler.

"Are you the only one who understands English?" he asks.

I glance at Secretary Choi Bo-gum. "Chairman Park's secretary is fluent, as well."

"You don't call him *Abeoji*?" he asks, looking surprised that I call my father by his title.

"In our culture, we use the formal titles and last names," I explain, and then I compliment him, "The few Korean words you've spoken you've pronounced well. Have you been learning Hangul?"

He lets out a chuckle, and it's such a happy sound I find myself wishing he would do it again.

"I can only say a couple of words. I've even watched Korean dramas hoping it will help me learn faster."

I begin to smile. "Which drama did you watch?"

He chuckles again, and the sound puts me more at ease. "I watched quite a few, but *Healer* and *The K2* were my favorite."

My smile widens even more. "I like those as well."

"Yeah?" He grins at me. "Because of the main actor?"

I nod and let out an awkward laugh. "Everyone loves him. He's a nice person."

"You have a beautiful smile," he suddenly says, and it makes me lower my eyes when I begin to feel self-conscious.

"Thank you," I whisper, and when he reaches for a glass of water, my eyes follow his hand until I can't see it any longer without having to look up.

His laughter sounds kind.

Please let him be a good person.

Lake

Even though this headache is killing me, I feel better after our short talk. Hell, I even made her smile.

"Lake," Mr. Reyes calls from the other side of the table, "Mr. Park will be leaving on Wednesday. Can you arrange a suite at the dorm for Miss Park to move into?"

Oh wow, he's leaving earlier than I expected.

"Yes, of course," I answer. Looking at Lee, I ask, "What time can I pick you up from the hotel?"

She darts a glance at me before she looks in the direction of Mr. Park, and I can't stop a frown from forming when the secretary talks with him for a moment before replying, "At twelve pm."

Mr. Park says something else, and then the secretary asks, "Chairman Park would like to know when you'll start working at CRC Holdings."

My eyes dart to Mr. Reyes, who responds for me, "Lake will only be active as a shareholder."

When the secretary translates the answer, the boring lunch transforms into something I've only seen in a drama.

Mr. Park shakes his head hard, and with a loud voice, starts saying, "No. No. No!"

He begins to ramble in Korean, which has me leaning closer to Lee. "What is he saying?"

She glances at me then back at Mr. Park, but begins to whisper, "He says you have to join the company. He won't invest unless you do. He feels his investment should be looked after by my husband."

"That was not the arrangement," Mr. Reyes says, his voice calm in comparison with Mr. Park's.

When Mr. Park begins to speak again, Lee whispers, "He wants it added to the contract that you'll work at CRC Holdings."

Before Mr. Reyes can reply, I say, "With all due respect, this is my future we're discussing. I'd like to say something."

Every pair of eyes settles on me, but I look directly at Mr. Park, and for once, he can't just glance over me. "Are you aware of the percentage of shares my family holds?"

"Chairman Park is adamant. He wants you working at CRC Holdings, or he would rather have his daughter marry Chairman Reyes' eldest son," the secretary says.

I can't keep the smile from forming around my lips as I shake my head. When I stand up, Mason and Falcon instantly rise to their feet as well. Locking eyes with Mr. Park, I say, "Decisions regarding CRC Holdings' future are all made in the boardroom, Mr. Park."

I'm well aware of the fact that I just insulted him by not using his title, and I pause a moment for that knowledge to sink in.

"I hold thirty percent." I gesture to Mason. "Mr. Chargill holds thirty percent." I bring my hand up, resting it on Falcon's shoulder. "Mr. Reyes holds ten percent. That gives us an overwhelming seventy percent voting right. We are a package deal, and Mr. Chargill will be the one to join CRC Holdings."

Somehow the secretary managed to listen to me and translate at the same time.

Damn, I need to learn Korean, so I can tell this man to go to hell in his own language.

"The Chairman asks what is stopping him from offering his daughter to Mr. Chargill."

I feel Mason's anger to my left, and glancing at him, I smile. "I've got this."

Taking a moment to gather my thoughts, I glance at Mr. Reyes first, and when he nods, my eyes go to Mr. Chargill. The corner of his mouth pulls up, and lastly, I look at my father.

"Speak your mind, son. I back whatever decision you make."

I lock gazes with Mr. Park. "CRC Holdings does not belong to one man. It belongs to three families. Out of the four sons, I am your only option."

"What the Chairman needs to realize," Mr. Reyes says, "is that the men in our families run CRC Holdings and have done so successfully for two generations. Our wives do not have a say in the business."

I button my jacket, and I feel Falcon move the chair from where it's right behind me. "Mr. Park." I wait for him to look at me. "CRC Holdings will not be intimidated. Our foundation isn't built on fear, it's built on loyalty. Consider this before you insult me again. I might be the quiet one, but that doesn't make me the weakest."

I step back and bow to the man. Rising up, I turn to Lee. "It was nice meeting and getting to talk to you, Park Lee-ann. If we don't meet again, I wish you a happy life."

She slowly rises to her feet as I begin to walk away, and I only take another four steps with Mason and Falcon flanking me when Mr. Park calls out, "Stop."

I only turn slightly and glance back at him.

He begins to chuckle, then says in perfect fucking English, "I wanted to make sure I was investing in the right company. We can sign the contract."

Not answering Mr. Park, I turn my gaze to Mr. Reyes. "Let me know the outcome, please."

"Will do. Go get some rest."

My eyes go to Lee, and for the first time, she's looking at me as if she actually sees me. She bows low, and I know it's a sign of great respect. When she straightens up, I lock eyes with her and smile before I turn and leave the dining area.

Chapter 3

Lake

When the valet brings our car, Falcon opens the door for me.

"Thanks," I murmur. I first shrug off my jacket and lay it over the back headrest. Loosening the damn tie, I throw it inside, then I unbutton the top two buttons of the dress shirt. When I take off the cufflinks, Falcon holds out his hand to take them, then drops them in his suit pocket.

I unbutton my right cuff and roll the sleeve up to beneath my elbow. While I'm doing the same with the left side and glancing up at Falcon, then at Mason, I say, "Well, that was fun."

Falcon's eyes rest intensely on me. "I don't like this one bit."

"Let's just call it off. I can find another investor," Mason offers.

"Mr. Cutler!"

Out of habit, my head darts in the direction of my name being called, and a wave of dizziness almost drags my ass down to the ground.

"Fuck, Lake!" Falcon snaps, and grabbing hold of my arm when I stumble back, he growls, "Sit your ass down before I have to pick you up off the damn ground."

I lean back against the side of the car, taking deep breaths while the dizzy feeling subsides.

When I'm able to look up, Lee apologizes, "I'm sorry." She bows again then says, "That was thoughtless of me. Are you okay?"

"Just whiplash," I explain. "Did you need something?"

When she drops to her knees right outside the main entrance of the country club, my lips part and a what-the-fuck expression settles on my face.

"I apologize for my father offending you."

"Please get up," I whisper while it feels like my heart is shrinking.

When she doesn't move, I straighten out and walk forward. Taking hold of her arm, I pull her up.

"Look at me," I say, and I have to take deep breaths to keep calm.

This is her culture.

Fuck, I hate her culture.

Slowly she tilts her head up until our eyes lock.

"Don't ever kneel in front of me again. I understand it's your culture, and I'll do my best to meet you halfway, but I won't stand for you kneeling."

She nods, and I can see she wants to say something.

I tilt my head to keep hold of her eyes. "Say what you're thinking."

"I didn't mean it as a sign of disrespect, Mr. Cutler," she whispers.

"I know." I lift my hand from her arm, resting it on the side of her jaw. "It's one of the biggest differences between us. To you, it's showing respect. To me, it's a sign of weakness. I don't want you to change who you are, just don't kneel to me." I begin to pull my hand away, then add, "Oh, and please call me Lake."

"You want to speak without honorifics?" Surprise ripples over her face.

"Yes, so is it okay if I call you Lee instead of your," I pull my hand back and gesture in the air, "you know, your whole name?"

The corners of her mouth begin to tip up, and she nods her head. "You may call me Lee."

Bringing my hand back to her arm, I give her a gentle squeeze. "I'll see you on Wednesday."

She nods and steps back, but keeps looking at me as I get into the backseat and before I close the door, she calls out, "I hope you feel better soon… Lake."

A huge smile spreads over my face. "Thanks, Lee."

The second Mason steers the Bentley away from the country club, I lie down and close my eyes, mumbling, "I swear I'm going to sleep right through to Wednesday."

"Well, that won't be a change in your daily activities at all," Mason mutters under his breath.

"Falcon, Mace is mean to me while I'm sick," I complain, a grin spreading over my face.

"Seriously? You're going to use the fucking whiplash against me for the next couple of days?" Mason grumbles.

"I'd be stupid not to," I chuckle. "It's not every day I get the chance."

"All jokes aside," Falcon says, glancing back over his shoulder. "That was a total shit storm back there."

"Yeah," I whisper.

"I was serious. I can find another investor. I've heard Indie Ink Publishing is looking to expand into a different market. The shareholders are young, and three of them live here in California."

"I'm not going to lie, that's a relief to hear. Let's see how things go." I place my forearm over my eyes, then add, "You should meet with them, though. Think how impressive it will be if you attend the next board meeting with a deal on the table."

"You're right. I'll set up a meeting with the three shareholders and see how that goes."

We fall silent for a couple of minutes, and I begin to drift off when Falcon says, "You didn't eat anything at lunch. Should we stop to pick up something?"

"No, I just want to sleep," I mumble.

"That's it," Mason growls, and he begins to switch lanes, "I'm taking you to the hospital."

Lifting my hand, I scowl at the back of his head. "Don't waste time. I'm fine."

"You have never said no to food. You're definitely not fine," Mason snaps.

Twenty minutes later, I'm glaring at Mason as he watches me with a smirk while a nurse checks my vitals.

"Everything seems normal," the nurse says. "I'll get a prescription for anti-inflammatories and a neck brace." She rambles off more things to which I just reply, "Thank you."

When I get the prescription, I shove it against Mason's chest. "It's your turn to get it filled out. I'll be in the waiting room."

"My turn?" he asks as I start to walk away.

"Yes, this is payback for Aspen. I'm also going to be stubborn and not take my meds," I call back to him but then the throbbing in the back of my skull increases, and I quickly add, "Hell no, get the meds so this damn headache can go away."

Chuckling, he smirks. "What happened to being stubborn?"

"It's the thought that counts," I mumble, making Mason laugh as he heads to the pharmacy.

As soon as the prescription is filled, I take the prescribed dosage, and under the hawk-eye supervision of Falcon, I strap the damn brace on. "Happy?"

Falcon smiles and pats my shoulder. "Good, boy."

I let out a burst of laughter but quickly stop. "I'm going to lose my sense of humor by the time I've recovered from this damn whiplash."

Lee

Feeling torn, I stare at the wall in my hotel suite, while I try to process everything that happened today.

Lake.

I really like his first name. I haven't spent a lot of time with him but after today… he made me feel like I matter.

Even though he was clearly not feeling well, he never failed to be courteous and kind. I find a smile forming around my lips when I remember the sound of his chuckle. It was deep and such a happy sound.

He doesn't want me kneeling.

When Chairman Park ordered me to formally apologize to Lake, it felt like a piece of my soul would die, and my pride received a death blow when I lowered myself to the ground. The act was the most shameful thing I've ever done.

But instead of accepting my apology, Lake pulled me to my feet and instructed me to never kneel again.

Chairman Park dishonored me, but Lake Cutler returned my lost pride to me with a gentle touch and a kind smile.

Who is this man?

Lifting my hands, I cover my face when hope hits me hard, making my heart quiver from the mere possibility that my life might not be as doomed as I first thought.

Can I dare hope Lake's really a good person?

I came here with the intent of making him break off the engagement, and now that I think about all the ways I planned to make it happen, I find myself resisting the very ideas which I've been fantasizing about for the past three months.

Maybe...

Maybe Lake is the solution and not the obstacle?

Or maybe I'm naive thinking a foreigner will help me to reunite with my mother.

Lake

Lying on the couch I'm practicing some Korean words and glancing at Mason's closed bedroom door, I call, "Mace!"

I wait for three seconds. "Mace!"

"What?" he yells back.

"Help!"

When he yanks the door open, with shampoo suds still in his hair and gripping a towel around his waist, I press my lips together so I won't burst out laughing.

"I'm thirsty," I whine, giving him the cute pleading look he can never say no to.

He walks into the living room, leaving a trail of wet footprints on the carpet. Glaring at the table, he growls, "You have water, OJ, and a fucking milkshake on the table. Pick one."

My lips begin to hurt from holding the laughter in and reaching over, I even pretend to stretch. "I can't reach any of them."

He stalks to the table, grabs the water bottle, and tosses it onto my chest. "You better find religion because it's only a matter of minutes before I kill you."

When he stalks back to his room, I call out, "Love you, buddy."

His door slams shut and I let out a chuckle as I grab the bottle from my chest and place it back on the table.

Falcon comes out of his room, laughing, "He's going to beat the shit out of you."

"I'm trying to see how far I can push him. I'm doing him a favor by teaching his impatient ass how to hold back."

Falcon sits down on the couch, shaking his head at me. "It's your funeral."

"How much damage can he do with a damn pillow?"

"True." Falcon leans back against the couch, then asks, "When are you going to arrange everything for Lee's arrival? You do remember you have to pick her up tomorrow?"

"It's all taken care of," I say, grinning at him.

"You haven't left that damn couch since your ass touched it on Sunday. When did you take care of it?"

"Preston. You know the assistant y'all stole from me?"

Falcon begins to chuckle. "You asked Preston to prepare a suite for a girl?"

"Yeah, what's wrong with that?"

Mason comes walking into the living room, shooting me a scowl before he sits down next to Falcon. His gaze goes to the unopened water bottle, and it makes him narrow his eyes, and then he grumbles, "For starters, Preston might be a genius, but he's senseless as fuck when it comes to women.

"He is? What makes you say that?" I ask, and I begin to sit up, feeling a little worried.

"He helped Layla and me prepare Kingsley's suite," Falcon says, and the grin on his face makes my worry grow. "What's the one thing Kingsley loves most?"

60

"Her candy stash?" I glance at Mason. "And him of course."

"Preston got rid of all the candy. When I asked him why, he said it's not healthy for her, and she's recovering. If I hadn't stopped him, Kingsley would've come home to a bowl of fruit with vitamins on the side."

I let out a bark of laughter. "You should've let him do that. I would've paid to see Kingsley's face."

"Wait, there's more," Falcon says. "He even ordered... shit, what were they called again?" he asks Mason.

"Expand-a-lung breathing fitness exerciser and a deep breathing lung exerciser," Mason mumbles. "The one had those balls in them, you have to try and blow to the top."

"Expand-a-lung." I begin to laugh. "Blowing balls."

Yeah, I wonder who's balls we're talking about here.

I crack up at the thought, and I have to grab hold of my stomach to try and breathe.

Falcon begins to chuckle, but Mason tilts his head, saying, "For someone who was dying ten minutes ago, you sure look fine right now."

"The healing power of laughter," Falcon, mutters before he chuckles again.

Mason nods and drawing his bottom lip between his teeth, he gives me a you-are-so-fucked look. "Keep laughing," he warns. "Meanwhile, Preston is converting Lee's suite into a fucking Buddhist temple."

I shoot up, the laughter disappearing at the speed of light. "He wouldn't."

Mason sits back and smiles. "I helped him carry a Feng Shui gong to the suite. He even had a miniature yin and yang zen garden because it's the symbol on South Korea's flag."

"In other words," Falcon says, "it's safe to say you're fucked."

Darting to my feet, I run for the door, and it has Mason and Falcon laughing their asses off. I rush down the stairs to the floor beneath ours and almost crash my way into Lee's suite, only to come to a sudden stop.

"Holy shit," I breathe as my eyes scan over the room. The left wall of the living room is covered in cherry blossoms.

In the middle of the floor, there's only a coffee table with two pillows on either side.

Preston comes out of the bedroom, and when he sees me, he smiles. "What do you think?"

I hear Kingsley snort behind me and glancing over my shoulder, I see Falcon and Mason standing with the girls. "You all just let him do this?"

Mason shrugs. "Payback for the past three days of having to be your bitch."

"My bitch?"

"Mace, I'm hungry. Mace, I'm bored. Mace, I'm thirsty," Mason gives a really bad impression of me.

I nod and taking a deep breath, I walk into the empty as fuck space and ask, "What happened to all the furniture?"

"You don't like it?" Preston asks. His shoulders slump, and he shoves his hands in his pocket. Scrunching his nose, he sniffs.

"I didn't say that," I say quickly, and darting forward, I place an arm around his shoulders. "I thought we could add a couple of more things."

Suddenly Preston looks up and grinning he says, "I'm just fucking with you."

I shove him away from me, but then rethink it, and when I move to slap him upside the head, he ducks and runs toward Mason, who's bending over from all the laughter.

I nod as I stare at my friends. "Well played."

"Come on, let's get to work," Layla says with a wide smile on her face.

They all leave me standing in the suite. "Where are you going?"

A moment later, Falcon and Mason carry a study desk in and place it by the window. Preston brings the chair.

Ten minutes later, I'm swallowing hard on the lump in my throat as I watch my friends transform the suite into nothing short of an idyllic space.

Indoor plants lend life to the cherry blossom art on the wall. I help move the coffee table and cushions to the side while Falcon and Mason bring in a couch.

"I figure if we leave the cushions on the couch, she can decide whether she wants to move them to the floor if she prefers dining in a more traditional way," Preston says.

"Huh?" Kingsley asks.

"You know, sitting on the floor at a coffee table," he explains.

"Oh." She gives Mason a what-the-hell-is-he-talking-about look.

"Some Koreans also prefer to sleep on the floor," Preston continues.

"By choice?" Kingsley asks, her eyes widening.

"Yes, they actually find it more comfortable."

"Yeaaahhh…. No way am I giving up my bed for the floor," she mumbles.

"Last night, you seemed fine with the floor," Mason mumbles under his breath.

When a dark frown settles on Kingsley's face, I bring a hand to my mouth and pretend to cough, "Run."

"Run?" Mason asks, and then Kingsley shoves her fists on her sides and raises an eyebrow at him.

"Seriously? You're going to tell our friends we bumped uglies on the floor?"

When I suck in a breath to laugh, I choke on a drop of spit flying down the wrong hole, and I'm close to sounding like I'm dying because I can't stop laughing while almost hacking up a lung.

Chapter 4

Lake

I drive the Bentley to pick up Lee, figuring she'll have a shitload of luggage.

When I get to the hotel, I expect to meet the Chairman and for the whole process to take a while, but when I walk into the lobby, Lee's already waiting.

I check the time to make sure I'm not late and seeing I still have fifteen minutes, I let out a relieved breath.

"Hi, why are you waiting down here?" I ask.

A look of confusion flashes over her face. "I was waiting for you. Is that wrong?"

"No." I tilt my head, then ask, "So I don't need to meet with your father?"

"The Chairman already left."

I used to think I'm one of the most patient people on this planet... until I met the Parks.

"What time did he leave?" I ask, already knowing I'm not going to like the answer.

"They left at five O'clock."

Which means I could've come much earlier.

"Do you still need to check out?" I ask, gesturing at the reception area.

"Oh no, we can leave. Secretary Choi took care of that."

"Is he still here?" I ask, thinking it's weird he didn't leave with Mr. Park.

Lee frowns while shaking her head. "No, he left with the Chairman."

"Hold on." I pull at the tie, loosening the damn thing. "Since what time have you been standing in this lobby?"

"Since five O'clock."

I stare at her until she lowers her eyes because I need a moment to breathe through the anger.

Seven fucking hours.

Keep calm, Lake. You can deal with this once she's settled into her suite.

"You must be exhausted. Where's your luggage?" I ask, glancing around for any sign of a luggage cart.

68

"Oh, right here." She turns around and picks up a suitcase.

"Is that all?" I ask, glancing around her like an idiot as if her petite body can hide a cart with luggage.

"I have a backpack too." She's starting to look at me like I've lost my mind, and then she asks, "Do you feel better after Sunday?"

Instantly a smile plays around my lips. "I'm completely healed, thanks for asking." I take the suitcase from her, and when she picks up the backpack, I take that as well and shrug it over my shoulder. "Let's get going."

"I can carry one of the bags," she offers, rushing to keep up with me, which has me shortening my steps.

"Let me be a gentleman and carry the bags."

When the valet brings the Bentley, I place the two bags on the backseat and open the door for Lee to climb in. She does a slight, quick bow before getting into the car.

Walking around the front, the niggling suspicion I've been feeling about Lee's text messages and the video calls grow into a full-blown concern.

I settle in behind the steering wheel, and when I look at her, and I notice she hasn't put on her safety belt, I don't think and reach over her.

"Eomeo!" she presses herself back against the seat, her eyes wide on me.

"Safety belt," I explain and grabbing it, I quickly pull it over her and click in place before I sit back in my seat.

"What does eomeo mean again?" I ask as I start the engine.

"Oh, my gosh, or something similar to that."

"Sorry if I startled you." I quickly smile at her before I pull away from the hotel.

Once I'm on the freeway, I glance at Lee and notice she's looking out the window, her face filled with fascination. It's the first time she looks relaxed.

Grinning, I pick up my phone and unlocking the screen, I press play on the playlist I've made just for this ride.

When the song starts, Lee's eyes snap to the radio, and she first listens to the intro before the most beautiful smile spreads over her face. "You listen to BtoB?"

I nod and smile back at her while turning up the volume.

I let out a breath when I feel the tension ease away. This is better. We have time to get to know each other without interference from our parents.

Lee

Hearing the familiar lyrics makes emotions explode in my chest. I can't stop smiling, while an overwhelming urge to cry pushes up my throat.

I stare out the window at the foreign landscape that looks like it goes on forever. Growing up on a small island surrounded by an ocean, and having a volcano and crater lake for a heartbeat, this country feels too big... too dry.

After a couple of songs, Lake turns the volume softer, then he asks, "You grew up near Seoul, right?"

I can't remember if Jo Yoon-ha told him where I lived, and not sure what to answer, I ask, "Didn't I tell you?"

"No, I just assumed that because your father is based in Seoul."

I wonder what he knows about my family. Does he know I was taken away from my home and mother?

Deciding to test him, I tell him the truth, "I lived on Jeju island with my mother."

"You did?" He glances at me with surprise on his face.

I nod and looking down at my hands where they're resting on my lap, my thoughts go to Mom.

I haven't spoken to her since last Thursday.

Jo Yoon-ha took the phone with her, so I won't be able to call Mom. I glance at the time on the dashboard, and seeing that it's thirty minutes past twelve, I minus sixteen hours for the time difference. Mom's been awake for thirty minutes already because she always gets up at four am.

I glance at Lake's phone, wishing I could borrow it. Just for five minutes. Just to hear Mom's voice.

"How was it growing up on an island?" Lake asks, pulling me out of my thoughts.

"I was free." Only after speaking the words, do I realize I actually said them out loud, and I scramble to

72

fix the mistake. "We lived on the outskirts of the city. All our neighbors were friendly, and we helped each other."

"What do you miss most about home?" he asks.

I keep my eyes on my hands when my sight begins to blur, and I take a deep breath while forcing the tears back.

"My mom."

I miss her scolding me because I'm late for work.

I miss her rushing me every morning so I wouldn't miss the bus for school.

I miss her calloused hands, rough from all the hard work.

"I miss gathering clams with her," I whisper as I get lost in my happy memories. "When the *Haenyeo* would go out to dive for abalone and shellfish, we would sit on the rocks and wait to see what they came back with."

It was the only time we sat still together.

Then I remember how Mom used to argue with them over the prices, and I let out a burst of laughter.

"My mom would argue with them all the way from the beach to market about the prices."

"And would she manage to get a lower price?" Lake asks.

I shake my head, letting out a soft chuckle. "No, but it didn't stop her from trying."

Lake

Listening to Lee while she tells me about her life, it only raises more questions for me. One of those questions is what she likes to do in her spare time. She told me she likes shopping, going to spas and horseback riding – the usual things the girls I grew up with liked doing.

It prompts me to ask, "Is that what you did in your spare time? Gathering clams?"

She's deep in thought when she answers, "There wasn't such a thing as spare time." A soft smile plays around her mouth. "We would get up at four in the morning, so I could help Mom prepare some of the foods we sold at our food stall. Then I'd get ready for school. After school, I'd go to the coffee shop for my six-hour shift. When I was done there, I'd go to the market and help Mom manage the stall, and we'd start packing up at eleven so we could be home by twelve."

Holy. Fuck.

"I miss it," she murmurs.

Three simple words, but they pack one hell of a punch. What sounds like a life of slavery to me is normal to her.

"Did you work because you wanted to?" I ask. I can't see anyone growing up with her family's kind of wealth, willingly working their asses off.

The question pulls her out of her thoughts, and her eyes dart to me.

I can see she's thinking of how to answer me, so I rephrase the question. "Didn't your father pay child support?"

Her features tense, and the happy glow she had a moment ago gets lost in the impassive expression.

"I only met him two years ago."

I want to pull over and stop the car. I want to drag all the answers out of her, but keeping my calm, I focus on the road as we approach the campus. But before I turn into the gates of Trinity, I ask, "Did you have a choice to come here?"

Chapter 5

Lee

"Did you have a choice to come here?"

It's such a straightforward question.

"Yes."

I had to choose between marrying you or having my mother sent away.

Mom can't speak any other languages, and the ways of the island are all she knows. She wouldn't survive outside of Korea.

And I can't bear the thought of not seeing her again.

Lake steers the car through two massive iron gates, and I glance around at the well-maintained grounds, and impressive buildings.

When he enters a parking area, my lips part because there are makes of cars I've never seen before.

After reversing into a parking bay, Lake switches off the engine. He unclips his safety belt, and I wait for him to finish before I begin to reach for my own, but our hands connect when he unclips mine as well. I quickly pull back, my fingers tingling the same way my arm and face did when he touched me on Sunday.

When he opens his door, and I begin to reach for my own, he says, "I'll get your door for you."

I watch as he climbs out and jogs around the front of the car.

As he opens the door for me, I slightly incline my head. "Thank you." I get out and the stupid heel I'm wearing twists under my foot. "Eomeo!" Stumbling forward and trying to regain my balance, I slam into Lake.

With wide eyes, I freeze until I realize I grabbed hold of his sides. I pull back so fast, my back hits the door jamb of the car.

Lake reaches for me, but stops midway, then asks, "Is it okay if I touch you? Especially when you're about to fall. I don't want to offend you or your traditions."

I nod, not able to meet his eyes as embarrassment burns in my chest.

Knowing I should say something, I gather my courage and lift my eyes to his. "It's not against my traditions." I pause but then quickly add, "I'm just not used to it."

"Being touched in general, or having a guy touch you?"

U-wa! How can he ask a question like that so bluntly?

It makes heat creep up my neck and settle in my face.

Then he adds, "If I do something that makes you feel uncomfortable, please tell me."

I step to the side and let out a burst of awkward laughter. "You're very direct." I press my hands to my cheeks because it feels like they're on fire, then I answer, "I was raised not to display affection publicly. Not that I'm saying you're affectionate. Ah..." stumbling over my words only makes everything feel so much worse, which leaves me whispering, "It's hard to explain."

"Take your time." His voice is filled with patience, and it makes me look up at him.

Meeting his kind eyes, I admit, "You're the first man I've interacted with like this."

A slight frown forms on his forehead. "You haven't dated before?"

I shake my head. "There wasn't time to date, and technically they were all boys."

Lake closes the door, saying, "I'll keep that in mind. Let's grab your bags and get you up to your suite."

When he has the bags out of the car, he turns and glances up at the buildings. "Welcome to Trinity Academy, Lee." Bringing his eyes back to me, he continues, "I really hope you'll be happy here."

"Thank you, Lake." I bow my head, appreciating the warm welcome.

We begin to walk out of the parking area, and I take the opportunity to glance around me. On the opposite side of the road, there's a park, and when a girl comes running out of one of the buildings, sprinting across the lawn while laughing because a man is chasing her, I stop, and can't prevent myself from staring.

"Noooo!" She shrieks when he catches up to her, and grabbing hold of her, he throws her over his shoulder. He slaps her backside, and my eyes almost pop out of my head.

"Mason! Put me down!" she yells while laughing out loud.

"Lee?"

I hear Lake's call, but I can't stop looking at them.

"Ne?" I answer.

"That's hangul for yes, right?" Lake steps into my line of sight, and I blink quickly.

"I'm sorry, what did you ask?"

He glances over his shoulder, and then he lets out a chuckle before mumbling, "Yeah, trust my friends to leave you with that for a first impression."

He gestures for me to walk, and when we cross the road, the constant hum of nervousness I've been feeling ever since we left Korea, becomes stronger until it feels like my empty stomach is nothing but a tight knot.

The couple I was watching comes walking toward us, and I recognize Mr. Chargill from the airport and Sunday's lunch. Bowing low, I say, "Good Afternoon, Mr. Chargill."

When I straighten up, Lake places his hand on my lower back. It's a soft touch and doesn't feel invasive.

"You can speak informally to Mason, and anyone else I introduce you to."

I glance up at Lake, and he gives me a reassuring smile.

"Yes, and you can call me Kingsley," the girl says, pulling my attention to her.

U-wa! I stare at her, having never seen her color eyes before.

She lifts a hand to her face. "Did I get chocolate all over myself again?"

"Oh, no!" I gesture to my own eyes. "I've never seen blue eyes before. They're so pretty."

"Aww... thank you!" Kingsley darts forward, which has me taking a sharp breath, and when she wraps an arm around my shoulder, I stand frozen for a moment before my shoulders relax.

I can feel this girl is good, and it makes me awkwardly lift my hand and place it on her back.

"Kingsley," Lake says, while grinning at her with an affectionate look I haven't seen before. "Lee's not used –"

Not wanting him to tell her to move away, because honestly, I feel safer with her than with a man, I quickly say, "She's a girl... it's different."

"What's different?" Kingsley asks, and when I look at her, she gives me a warm smile.

"In Korea, it's frowned upon for a man and a woman to be affectionate in public places, but for two women... I mean friends, it's a normal thing to see," I try my best to explain.

Instantly a mischievous grin spreads over Kingsley's face. "Y'all heard that right. Only Layla and I get to hug Lee." She wraps her other arm around me, giving me a tight hug, and although it's not something I'm used to, I appreciate the gesture.

"Welcome, Lee." She pulls back and then claps her hands excitedly. "Wait until you see your suite!" She begins to bounce, grabs my hand, and then I'm yanked inside the building.

Lake

"Sorry, buddy," Mason says as we stare after the girls. "There's no stopping Kingsley when she's excited. I'm afraid she might traumatize Lee before the day is over."

I have a special place in my heart for Layla and Kingsley, who are like little sisters to me. But watching Kingsley embrace Lee without any reservations, only makes me love the girl more.

"I think Kingsley is the just person to make Lee feel at home here," I give my opinion.

Mason grabs the backpack from my shoulder, and we walk toward the girls where they're waiting for the elevator.

When we step inside, and Mason takes hold of the back of Kingsley's neck, pulling her to his side so he can press a kiss to her hair, I don't miss how Lee takes a step closer to me.

I'm totally taking it as a good sign that she feels somewhat safe with me.

The idea of *somewhat* flies right out the doors as they open and Falcon, Layla, and Preston, yell, "Welcome!"

Lee darts in behind me, which has Mason pushing Kingsley out of the elevator while he gestures for the group to cut it.

I place the suitcase in the door so they won't close, then turn to Lee, who's peeking down the hallway, watching my friends walk toward her suite.

"It's all a bit overwhelming, isn't it?" I ask, and taking a chance, I place my hand on her shoulder.

She nods while swallowing. "I'm sorry. I didn't expect to hear yelling when the doors opened."

"They're all just excited to meet you," I explain.

She takes a breath and lifts her chin with determination on her face. "I'll try hard to adapt faster to the way you do things here."

"You're doing a great job already," I encourage her.

Then she does the cutest thing I've ever seen. She holds up her small fist and smiling, she says, "Fighting!"

I've heard the term in the dramas I've watched, and know it has a similar meaning to you can do this or good luck.

I imitate her gesture and grinning, I say, "Fighting."

It has her smile widening, and for the first time, it shows in her eyes, making them sparkle like black diamonds.

I move my hand and placing my arm around her shoulder, I nudge her out of the elevator. I feel the need to warn her as I pull the suitcase behind us. "There might be some more hugging, and when they get really excited, they all talk at once."

"Okay." She nods, taking in the information like a dry sponge.

"Another thing, if you hear Mason and Kingsley snapping at each other, don't worry. It's the way they express their love for each other."

"Okay."

I grin down at her because somehow I've crossed over from being the strange, new guy, to being the only one she knows.

"Mr. Chargill's first name is Mason. His girlfriend is Kingsley, with the blue eyes," she quickly checks with me to see if she got it right.

"Yes." I pull her to a stop outside the door by the shoe cabinet Preston ordered for her. "You're going to meet Layla, she's Falcon's girlfriend."

"Falcon. Is that Mr. Reyes?"

I nod. "The other guy is Preston. I think he's most excited to meet you."

"Why?" she asks, her eyes widening slightly.

"He's really clever, and since he heard you were coming, he's been studying everything about Korea."

"Okay." She instantly relaxes, then glances at the door.

"Oh, Preston also got a shoe cabinet for you."

I step out of my shoes and place them with the others, and when I turn back to Lee, there's an emotional look on her face.

She steps out of her heels and places them next to mine. When she shuts the cabinet doors, she rests her hand on top of it, tilting her head to the side.

"Is everything okay?" I ask.

She takes a deep breath before she turns to me and nods. "I'm just touched by the consideration you and your friends are showing me. I didn't expect any of it."

"Are you ready?" I ask, just to make sure. I don't want to push her too fast.

"I'm ready."

"Fighting," I whisper, which has her smiling again.

When she steps into the suite, Kingsley begins to bounce with excitement, clapping her hands. "Do you like it?"

"Damn, woman!" Mason growls. "Give her time to actually look around."

"Shut up," she mumbles back at him.

An amused chuckle sounds up from next to me, and I take a step to the side so I can lean against the wall while I watch Lee's reaction to everything.

Preston darts forward and bowing at the waist, he says, "Annyeonghaseyo. Mannaseo bangapsseumnida."

Lee's smile softens to a grateful look as she bows. "Annyeonghaseyo." When she straightens up, she switches back to English, which is good because saying hello, it's nice to meet you just about covers the extent of what I've learned when it comes to complete sentences. "It's nice to meet you too. Thank you for the shoe cabinet."

"You're welcome. I've ordered a grill so we can have Korean BBQs, and I wasn't sure which beauty products you prefer, so I got a variety. Just let me know if there's something else you'd like from Korea, and I'll order it for you."

When Preston stops to take a breath, there's absolute silence as Lee just stares at him, a look of awe on her face.

Then Kingsley asks, "Why don't you order stuff like that for us?"

Preston frowns at her. "What could you possibly need. You have enough candy in your suite to last me an entire lifetime."

I smile because it's really good seeing Preston come out of his shell.

"What beauty products did you get?' Kingsley asks, and I notice how she keeps sneaking glances at Lee, giving her time to gather her emotions.

"Everything," and lifting his hands, he begins to tick the names of one by one, "Dr. Jart, Klairs, Missha, Sulwhasoo, and Laneige."

"Damn," Mason mumbles, "you sure you didn't miss anything?"

Preston shrugs off Mason's comment, and when he turns his attention to Lee, I dart forward. "Before you continue, let me introduce her to Falcon and Layla."

I gesture to Falcon, but Lee's eyes go straight to Layla, and her lips part in wonder while she murmurs, "U-waaaaa… ye-ppeo."

"She says you're pretty," Preston goes ahead and translates as if he's spoken the damn language all his life and didn't just start learning it.

"Show off," I mumble under my breath.

Layla walks closer and smiles at Lee. "It's nice to meet you. Is it okay if I call you Lee?"

Lee nods still transfixed with Layla, then she says, "I haven't seen anyone with such light hair and skin before. You're so beautiful."

Layla grins at Lee, totally basking in the damn spotlight, and then she says, "You're just as pretty. How do you get your skin looking so smooth? I need some beauty tips."

"Now we're talking," Kingsley adds.

I throw my hands up in the air at the guys. "Well, I guess that's their way of telling us to take a hike."

"Hike? Where? I'm not the outdoor sports type," Preston begins to ramble.

"He meant we need to get our asses out of the suite so the girls can bond," Mason grumbles.

Chapter 6

Lee

Falcon hugs Layla, pressing a kiss to her mouth, while Mason pulls Kingsley to his side, saying, "I'll see you at dinner. Have fun."

The men all begin to move toward the door, and it has me darting forward so I can catch up with them.

"Thank you so much." The words explode over my lips, and I wish I knew a way to express how grateful I am. I expected to see another room like the one at the hotel.

I meet Preston's eyes and hoping he'll understand, I bow. "Jeongmal gomapsseumnida."

"Chunmaneyo," he replies to my formal thank you.

They begin to leave again, and I move toward Lake. Touching his arm to get his attention, I smile nervously when he turns to me.

I take another step closer, then whisper, "I'm embarrassed to ask this, but is there a phone I can use to call my mother?"

I'm willing to sacrifice all my pride just so I can hear her voice again. I'm so desperate I'll even go down on my knees and beg if I have to.

"Of course," he says, and reaching for my hand, he pulls me deeper into the room to a desk standing by the window. He points to a phone and the numbers printed above the keypad. "These are the numbers for the campus."

I forget about Lake holding my hand because I'm filled with intense relief, knowing I have a way to contact my mom.

Then he frowns and looks at me. "What happened to your phone?"

"I don't have one," I automatically answer, but I quickly realize my mistake when his frown darkens.

"Who's phone did you use for us to text?"

It's too late to think of a lie now, so I answer honestly, "Jo Yoon-ha's."

Lake glances to the other girls, and without having to say anything, Layla and Kingsley walk to the door. "We'll be right outside."

I lower my eyes to where he's still holding my hand, wondering how much trouble I just got myself into.

When the door closes behind the two girls, Lake tilts his head. "Look at me, please."

An awful feeling of apprehension fills my chest, but I gather my courage and lift my eyes back to his.

"You didn't send any of those texts, did you?"

I swallow hard and shake my head.

A smile flashes over his lips, but there's nothing happy about it. Instead, it makes him look worried. "So, you don't know anything about me?"

I read the messages before every video call, but I can't recall the details. I only remember the shame I felt because of the things Jo Yoon-ha said.

Owing him an answer, I shake my head again.

He pulls his hand away, and I let mine fall back to my side.

Maybe he'll tell me to go home now.

Instead of feeling insulted and demanding I leave, Lake's mouth curves into a gentle smile, and he inclines his head, "Hi, Park Lee-ann. I'm Lake Cutler."

My heart fills with gratitude because he's showing consideration for me as an individual. It makes me feel like I matter, and that's something I haven't felt in a long time.

"Hi, Lake," I greet him back. It's hard to swallow the overwhelming emotions down, but I push through, adding, "You're different from what I expected, and it's really nice to meet you."

Lake

I'm always the one telling Mason to stop talking with his fists and to use words, but right now, I wish Park Je-ha was still in California so I could beat the shit out of him.

And that mistress of his. She better pray she never sees me again.

I feel insulted that they thought I was so stupid, and I'd never find out the truth.

My suspicions were right.

I was right about the difference in tone between the text and the video calls and the handprint on her arm. Fuck, let's not forget her entire past and the fact that she only met her father two years ago.

I have a bad feeling things are going to get a hell of a lot worse before they get better.

Locking eyes with her, I ask again, "Was it your choice to come to America? Did you agree to the marriage?" She remains quiet for a moment, and it has me adding, "Please tell me the truth."

"I have to respect the Chairman's decisions."

That's enough to tell me she didn't have any choice in the matter. There are so many questions I want to ask her, but I settle for asking her the most important one, "Do you want to go home?"

Emotion flashes over her face, and it feels like her entire being is screaming yes, but still, she whispers, "No."

I take a deep breath and walk a couple of feet away from her. Rubbing my hands over my face, I try to think what I'm going to do next.

I force a smile to my face, the one I've used many times before to fool those around me, except Mason and Falcon, then I turn to look at her. "Do you want to stay, Lee? Do you want to get to know me?"

"Yes." The word sounds like a reflex instead of a choice she made, and she must see the doubt on my face because she adds, "You've only been kind to me."

Are they holding something against her to force her into this marriage?

The question shudders through me, making me feel perplexed and honestly a little sick.

I glance to the side, and when my eyes land on the phone, a thought creeps into my mind.

"Your mother." As I say the words, I look back to her, and it's just in time to see the longing in her eyes before she schools her face again.

No. They wouldn't go that far, would they?

"You wanted to call her," I say and gesture to the phone.

Her eyes jump between me and the phone before she takes a step forward, and when she reaches for the earpiece, I notice how her hand trembles.

She dials the number and waits for the call to connect.

"Eomma?" Relief crashes over her, and it's so intense I can actually feel it.

I walk to the couch and sit down. Even though I don't understand the language, I can hear happiness mixing with sadness in every word she speaks.

I need to talk to Falcon and Mason about all of this. Lee must be exhausted from waiting in that damn lobby for seven hours, so I don't think she'll mind if I leave.

I close my eyes and take a deep breath.

Calm down. Take a moment and calm down.

While Lee talks to her mother, I walk to the door and opening it, I let out a chuckle when I see Layla and Kingsley sitting on the floor in the middle of the hallway.

"Are you done?" Kingsley asks, quickly climbing to her feet, and then she pulls a face. "Ahhh... my leg fell asleep."

Layla moves closer to me, and the moment our eyes meet, she whispers, "What's wrong?"

I shake my head and smile at the girls. "Could you do me a favor?"

"Anything." Kingsley limps closer, then shakes her leg as if she's a dog, and it makes the smile on my face turn into a real one.

"When I leave, can you ask Lee what she would like to eat and then have it brought to her suite?"

"We'll get her settled, fed, and…" Kingsley pauses, clearly having run out of words.

"We've got everything covered," Layla says.

"Thanks." I give them a grateful smile. "Just give me five more minutes with her."

Walking back into the suite, I hear Kingsley ask Layla, "What are you in the mood to eat?"

"Aren't you having dinner with Mason?" Layla asks.

"Hoes before bros… or something like that."

"Chicks before dicks," Layla laughs.

Trying not to crack myself up, I stare at them, and their laughter quickly fizzles out. "Please don't say stuff like that in front of Lee."

Kingsley wags her eyebrows at me. "I'm going to teach her everything I know."

"Yeah, that's what I'm afraid of," I mumble and hearing Lee hang up behind me, I show the girls five minutes with my hand then shut the door.

Walking to where Lee's still standing by the desk, I say, "I'm going to let you get settled. Layla and Kingsley will help you."

She nods with a smile on her face, then she asks, "What do you do to show someone you're grateful?"

I actually have to think about it. Everything is just second nature for me.

"There's the basic thank you. If you're friends, you could hug them. It actually depends on how big the favor was that they did for you."

"It's very big," she says. "I was really worried about my mother."

And just like that, she melts my heart. I feel a rush of compassion mixed with an intense need to protect this girl, spread through me.

"You don't have to thank me, Lee."

She lowers her head for a moment, and I hear her take a couple of deep breaths, and then she darts forward. I instinctively lean into her when she reaches up, wrapping her arms around my neck.

Placing an arm around her waist, and feeling her body so close to mine reminds me that she's not just a girl in need of help, but also the woman I've come to care for.

The hug is only for a couple of seconds, and then she pulls back.

"You're fine with Layla and Kingsley spending time with you, right?"

She nods, and a shy look settles on her face, coloring her cheeks pink.

Grinning like a damn idiot, I reach out, and when I cup her cheek, her eyes fly to mine. "I'll go get you a phone and bring it by later. Is there anything else you need?"

She shakes her head, and it makes her soft skin brush against my palm.

"Layla and Kingsley have my number. If you think of anything while you're unpacking, just have them call me."

"Okay."

I drop my hand to my side and look at her for a second longer before I walk to the door.

"Lake," she calls after me, and when I glance over my shoulder, she continues, "Thank you… a lot."

"You're welcome." I smile at her one last time before I let myself out of the room.

"Finally," Kingsley groans as she gets up from the floor again. "Ah, crap. Now my other leg's asleep."

Chuckling, I shake my head as I walk down the hallway. "Thanks, ladies. I owe you."

Chapter 7

Lee

The instant Lake leaves, I cover my face with my hands, taking deep breaths.

I know there's a lot I should be worried about, but right now, I'm just too relieved to care about any of it. Even though Mom sounded tired as always, it was so good to hear her voice.

When I asked her if everything was okay, she rambled on and on about the daily life on Jeju.

I could smell the ocean air she was breathing.

I could feel the wind I heard blowing over the line.

It feels as if my soul has been refreshed after the call.

I drop my hands from my face when I hear the door open, and again I'm shocked by how beautiful Layla is. I saw a couple of people who were light-haired and fair-skinned when we walked through the airport, but not up close. Not like this. Her hair looks like it's been spun from gold, and her skin can rival any pearl in the world.

"We should order food first," Kingsley says as she sits down on the couch. "What do you like to eat, Lee?"

Unconsciously I place a hand over my stomach. I haven't eaten since yesterday afternoon and could really eat half my weight in Tteokbokki.

I've also learned most of the food here tastes bland and oily, and I just can't stomach it.

"Do you have anything similar to ramen or any kind of noodles? Or rice?"

"I think we should walk over to the restaurant and talk to the chef. I'm sure he can whip up something for you," Layla offers.

"He won't mind, will he?" I ask, not wanting to inconvenience anyone.

"He doesn't mind," Kingsley answers. "I have the restaurant add new toppings to my pizza every other day. Oh, did I tell you?" She glances at Layla. "I got them to make me a chocolate pizza."

"Just chocolate, right?" Layla asks, pulling a face.

"Yeah, but I think it would taste even better with pineapple."

Layla shakes her head, then brings her eyes to me. "Don't eat any food she gives you."

I smile, and I have to admit, I envy the friendship they share.

"We can get it to go then eat here while we unpack everything."

I follow the two girls out, but then Kingsley turns around and jogs back to where the coffee table is. She picks up a card and waves it in the air as she runs back to us. "We almost forgot the keycard. Trust me, you do not want to forget this in the suite when you go out. It took me hours to get a new one."

When we close the door behind us, Kingsley shows me how to use the card to open the door again before handing it over to me.

"Thank you." I don't have any pockets to put it in, and the thought makes me glance down at my dress. Then I look at the comfortable clothes Laya and Kingsley are wearing, and I ask, "Can I change quickly?"

Kingsley nods. "We should've thought of that first."

I open the door, and we all go back inside. "The bedroom's through there with an ensuite bathroom."

"Thank you." I grab my bags and walking into the bedroom, I come to a sudden halt when I see the futon bed.

"Is everything okay?" Layla asks.

Glancing over my shoulder, I smile. "Yes."

I hurry inside and set the bags down. I open the suitcase and take out a pair of jeans and a t-shirt.

Suddenly I hear a man's voice saying, *'Excuse me, but I'm afraid someone is endeavoring to contact you telephonically. Shall I tell them to fuck off?'*

I dart up and to the door, and when I see Kingsley answering her phone, I let out a chuckle. That's the weirdest ringtone I've ever heard.

"Lee's just changing, then we're going to get something to eat." She makes an ah-huh sound every couple of seconds before saying, "Tell him not to worry. I'll text you everything."

When she ends the call, she gets up from the couch and smiles at me. "Go change in the bathroom quickly while Layla and I unpack everything. That way, we can get it done now, and we can just hang out."

"Okay." I walk to the bathroom and closing the door, I quickly take off the dress. I splash water on my face and wash my hands before drying both. When I'm done getting dressed in the comfortable clothes, I feel much better.

Lake

Mason's phone starts beeping like crazy, which has me leaning closer so I can see what Kingsley's texting.

She needs everything. LIKE EVERYTHING.

Oh, my God. Look at this.

A photo comes through showing, two dresses, one pair of worn shoes, a pair of jeans, two t-shirts, and something that looks like it was made from tent material.

I sit back in my chair and close my eyes. "It feels like someone's trying to see how far they can push me before I lose my shit."

We came to get a phone for Lee and stopped for something to eat, so Preston could load all the necessary apps on it. I gave the guys a rundown of everything I know, and we're trying to come up with a plan.

"I'll give Rhett Daniels from Indie Ink Publishing a call so we can set up a meeting for next week," Mason says, and it makes me feel a little better.

"I hope it works out so I can tell Park Je-ha where he can shove his investment," I grumble.

"What else do you need us to do?" Falcon asks.

I shake my head. "You both still need to wrap things up with Serena and Clare. I'll handle the rest, once I can figure out what that entails."

"You can't just ask her?" Mason asks.

"No." I let out a heavy breath. "It turns out I've been texting with the damn mistress." I lean forward and place my elbows on the table, and covering my face with my hands, I mumble, "It feels like I've been violated by a sugarless mommy."

Falcon busts out laughing, spraying me with the sip of soda he just took.

"Noooo!" I shake my hands to get rid of the drops before I grab a napkin. "You're so lucky I had my hands in front of my face."

Then I hear a snort next to me. I glare at Mason, watching him try to cover his eyes with a hand while his whole body shakes with laughter.

"What's a sugarless mommy?" Preston mumbles, not taking his eyes off the phone in his hands.

Falcon cracks up and in the process, whacks a glass off the table.

A waitress rushes over and quickly begins to clean up the mess.

"I'm sorry," I say to her. "I'm still trying to teach them how to behave in public. You know," I let out a heavy sigh, "it's not easy being a single parent and raising three kids on my own."

Mason almost explodes next to me when the waitress gives me a what-the-fuck-are-you-talking-about look. With a huge smile on my face, I watch him laugh.

After Falcon and Mason calm down, I say, "You guys ready to go shopping?"

"I'll never be ready, but let's do this," Mason comments.

Preston hands me the phone. "All done. I can go get toiletries. You know, shampoo and stuff."

Mason places his hand on Preston's shoulder, nodding. "I second that idea. Don't forget the pads and shit."

"The what?" Preston blinks, looking like his brain's about to fry a circuit.

"You should come with us," Falcon says, pulling Preston away from Mason. "We'll start with underwear first."

I rub my hands over my face taking a deep breath. "This is going to be a long afternoon."

Mason pats me on the back. "I'm so glad you finally have a girlfriend." He grins at me.

"You're going to get back at me for all the shit I gave you, right?" I ask, grinning at him.

"You bet."

When we walk into a boutique, Falcon almost has to drag Preston to where the bras are. "What size do you like?"

"How would I know. I don't wear them," Preston answers, his cheeks already bright red.

"Come on, work with us here," Mason says as he goes to stand on the other side of Preston. "Do you like them big, or a handful, or a mouthful."

108

I cover my mouth when Preston looks like he's about to have a seizure. Then he mumbles, "Normal size ones."

I snort and quickly cover it up by faking a cough.

Falcon grabs a lace bra in one of the bigger sizes. "How about this size? You can bury your face between them."

"Dear Lord," Preston groans, and the pained expression on his face has me cracking up.

I walk to the smaller sizes and take five comfortable looking ones.

"How do you know her size?" Mason suddenly asks.

I make sure they're all the right size, then answer, "I hugged her."

Mason grins at me, "What? Do you have ta-ta sensors in your chest?"

"Ta-ta?" Falcon asks.

"That's what Kingsley calls them. Kinda grew on me."

I wag my eyebrows at the guys, "Told you, I'm special."

I get some underwear then go set them down on the counter so I can move onto the clothes. Soon Mason and Falcon give up on teaching Preston about breast sizes, and they also jump in, grabbing clothes until the poor shop attendant looks like she's overheating from trying to keep up with us.

After paying and giving her the address so they can have it all delivered, we walk out of the boutique and glancing up, and down the street, I say, "Next is toiletries. Are you guys ready?"

"Let's do this," Mason says, looking like he's on an unstoppable roll.

"And you said you hated shopping," I mumble under my breath. "You're worse than the girls."

He darts my way, which has me running down the street. When he comes after me, I start to yell, "Help! There's a madman after me. Help!"

"Shut the fuck up," Mason shouts from behind me.

I only make it around to the corner before he grabs hold of my shirt, yanking me backward. I take a breath to yell again, but he slaps his hand over my mouth.

"Shut up," he says while laughing. "People are going to call the police."

A couple of seconds later, Preston comes jogging toward us, "Falcon can't walk."

"Why?" I ask, and when I glance up the street, I crack up laughing when I see Falcon leaning against a display window, trying to keep himself up while he laughs so hard he can't even make a sound.

"He's going to piss himself," Mason chuckles.

"Yeah, then the police are totally going to buy my madman story." Mason wacks me upside the head. "And now I can add abuse."

Mason is midway between Falcon and me, when he stops and shouts, "Let's get Falcon so we can go buy tampons."

"Dear Lord," Preston mumbles, but at least he's smiling.

"You've leveled up. Good for you," I say, patting him on the shoulder.

"Leveled up to what?" he asks, coming after me as I walk toward Falcon.

Chapter 8

Lee

Kingsley introduced me to Chef Anand, who didn't look very friendly, but he's making ramen for us, so I really don't care.

A waiter places little ceramic chopstick rests on the table, and then sets down the chopsticks. When he comes back with a tray of side dishes, and I actually recognize them, I cover my mouth with surprise. "Daebak!"

I glance up to thank him, but he smiles, saying, "Chef Anand apologizes for not being able to serve you kimchi with today's meal. He's prepared a spicy cabbage salad instead." The waiter gestures to the dishes as he names them, "Pa-jun with scallions. Gyeran-mari, we've substituted the seaweed with spinach. And lastly, sigeumchi namul."

I bow my head, totally overwhelmed by their kindness. "Thank you."

The waiter comes back out with three bowls of ramen. After he sets one down in front of me, I almost cry with relief just from how good it looks and smells.

"Jal meogeosseumnida," I whisper before I pick up my chopsticks.

"What did you just say?" Layla asks.

"I will eat well. It's like saying thank you for the food."

"How do I hold these things?" Kingsley asks.

"Position them like this in your hand." I show them how I hold mine. "I use my middle finger to move the bottom one, but go with whichever finger works best for you."

They both try and manage to get a bite of noodles into their mouths.

Not able to hold out any longer, I begin to eat, and I close my eyes as the rich, spicy taste hits my tongue.

"Oh my gosh," Kingsley moans. "It's burning the crap out of my mouth, but it's so good."

Out of habit, I reach for a gyeran-mari, and placing it in Kingsley's bowl, I say, "Try this. It's egg roll with vegetables in it."

She takes a bite and then moans again while gesturing to Layla to try one.

I smile as I watch them enjoy the food while shoveling my own ramen into my mouth as fast as I can.

After we're done eating and the waiter comes to clear the table, I stand up and ask, "Can I see Chef Anand for a moment?"

"Of course."

"I'll be right back," I say to the girls before I follow the waiter to the kitchen.

"Chef, a customer would like a moment of your time," the waiter calls into the busy kitchen.

When Chef Anand comes out, I bow at the waist. "Jeongmal gomapsseumnida." Coming back up, I quickly translate it, "Thank you very much for the meal."

Unlike before, where he looked grumpy, a smile pulls at his mouth. "You're welcome. I'll make sure the kitchen carries the right stock for your meals."

"Thank you." I incline my head again before I walk back out to where the girls are waiting.

"Let's go," Kingsley says, "I need to lie down and just digest everything for a while."

There are some guys coming into the restaurant, so I fall back and move in behind Layla as we leave.

"Eomeo!" The word rushes from me when someone grabs hold of my wrist.

"I haven't seen you around here before," A guy says, stepping closer until he's in my personal space.

I try to pull my arm free, but it only makes him tighten his grip.

Glancing to where Layla and Kingsley are, I see that they haven't noticed I'm not with them.

"Let go of my arm," I say as I look back up to the guy.

He ignores my request and says, "You're a pretty little thing. Are you old enough to be in this Academy?"

Lifting my chin, I ask him one more time, "Let go of my arm."

He circles his fingers around my wrist. "Look at this. She's so fucking small. I'd probably break her in half with my dick."

While he doesn't have a good grip, I yank my arm free and slightly bending my knees, I focus all my strength in my legs and jumping, I twist my body in the air. Pushing my left leg out, my heel connects with the side of his head.

Landing back on my feet, I watch as he staggers back, falling on his butt while shaking his head.

"Fuck," one of the guys he's with whispers.

I glare at them before I begin to walk away, mumbling, "Next time, let go when I ask nicely."

I stop when I see Layla and Kingsley watching me with absolute shock on their faces.

Maybe I should've asked a third time before kicking him.

I'm still second-guessing myself when Kingsley slowly lifts her hands and begins to clap. "That's the best thing I've seen in my entire life."

Layla begins to nod. "You have to teach us how to do that."

Feeling relieved that I haven't broken any rules by defending myself, I catch up with them, and say, "I can teach you a couple of kicks and hits. I'm not too good, though."

"Girl, if I tried kicking anyone like that, I'd be the one flat on my butt," Kingsley comments as she hooks her arm through mine.

Lake

"Dude, I'm telling you. She did this flying twirly thing in the air and kicked him so hard he went back a couple of feet before falling on his butt," Kingsley says with way too much excitement.

"Hold up." I get back up from the couch, and looking at Lee, I ask, "Someone grabbed you? Where? Who?"

Lee shrugs and holds her left wrist out for me. I take hold of her hand and brush my thumb over the red mark it left on her skin.

117

I let go of her hand as anger begins to burn through my chest.

"He's just some junior," Kingsley says, gesturing a hand as if it doesn't matter who it was.

"Kingsley, who?" I snap, and this time the angry look on my face gets her attention.

"George Thompson," she finally spits the name out.

I pull my phone out of my pocket and call the office. When reception answers, I say, "It's Lake. Which room is George Thompson in?"

"Lake," Falcon says, getting to his feet. "Let's talk first."

I shake my head at him.

"The Pink Star, room 202, Sir."

I end the call and stalk toward the door.

"Lake, wait," Mason calls after me.

They catch up to me as I head for the stairs, too worked up to stand still in an elevator right now.

"Lake, take a second to calm down first," Falcon says.

"He's past the point of calming down," Mason murmurs.

My heartbeat begins to beat heavy in my chest, sending a surge of adrenaline through my body as I cross the road to The Pink Star. I take the stairs up to the second floor and stop in front of room 202.

I bang a fist on the door, and when the door opens, I only have enough restraint to ask, "George Thompson?"

"Yeah?"

My fist connects with his jaw, and as he staggers back, I move forward. I grab hold of his shirt and let my knuckles slam into his cheek. The blow makes him sag to the floor, and I go down on one knee because I'm not done yet.

I only start to feel calmer when my fist meets his face for the fifth time. "If you ever touch her again, I will kill you."

I shove him back against the floor as I get up, my breaths exploding over my lips.

Covering the side of his face with a trembling hand, he mumbles around the blood, "Who?"

Stalking out of the room, I walk until I reach the stretch of lawn between the dorms and the library. Pressing the heels of my hands to my eyes, I take deep

119

breaths so I can calm down totally before I go back into our dorm.

I feel Falcon and Mason behind me, and the second I go down to my knees, they're right beside me.

"Take a deep breath," Mason begins to say in such a calm voice, it gets through the anger. He places his hand on my chest, then repeats the words, "Take a deep breath."

When my breathing begins to slow down, he wraps his arms around me. "I've got you. I've got you, buddy."

I take another couple of breaths before I say, "I'm good."

Falcon helps me up while Mason climbs to his feet. My shoulders sag, and shame hits me like a tidal wave. Bringing my eyes to Mason's, I say, "I snapped at Kingsley."

"She won't hold it against you," he assures me, his face still torn with worry.

"I'm sorry," I whisper, and then I look down at my hands and seeing the blood on them, makes me feel sick to my stomach.

Falcon pulls me into a hug, brushing his hand repeatedly over my back. "It was bound to happen. You had to deal with a lot today."

I shake my head against his shoulder.

"It's nothing we can't fix," he says, and pulling back, he frames my face with his hands. "You feeling better?"

I nod, and when he presses a kiss to my forehead, I let out a bark of laughter. "Now you're pushing it."

He smiles at me. "Anything to hear you laugh."

Knowing what I have to do now, I turn around and take a deep breath before I walk back to Lee's suite.

As soon as I step inside the living room, I go directly to Kingsley and wrapping my arms around her, I whisper, "I'm sorry I raised my voice at you."

She hugs me back, nestling her face against my chest. "It's okay. I should've answered you when you asked the first time."

I shake my head and tighten my grip on her before I let her go. Catching her eyes, I ask, "We're good, right?"

"Of course. Pfft. Like I would let something so small get between us when I had to deal with his grumpy ass for months," she says, jabbing a thumb in Mason's direction.

"I'm never going to hear the end of it," Mason grumbles, leaning back against the wall.

"Aww…" Kingsley coos, walking toward him, "but I still love you." The second the words leave her mouth, she freezes, and her eyes widen with surprise. "Oops." She shrugs and looking awkward, she makes a run for the door.

"You can't take that back," Mason yells as he sets off after her.

"And that's officially the weirdest and most random declaration of love I've ever seen," I mutter.

"I have to agree," Falcon says, holding out his hand to Layla. "Let's go, my rainbow."

I wait for him to close the door behind them before I turn to Lee.

"I'm just going to use your bathroom quickly," I say, and go to wash my hands. I didn't close the door behind me, but I'm still surprised when Lee follows me inside.

Pointing to the closed toilet, she says, "Sit."

I listen and sitting down I watch as she wets a facecloth. She squeezes the water out and then kneels down in front of me. Picking up my left hand, she begins to clean the blood off.

The corner of her mouth lifts. "I used to get into many fights when I was twelve. It was hard to control my temper."

"I can't imagine that," I admit.

Her lips stretch into a wide smile. "That's when I learned kung fu. I learned how to direct my emotions into healthier things, like work and helping my mom. It helped me find inner peace and patience."

I love hearing her voice. It's tranquil and soothing.

"Anger is a healthy and natural emotion. It's when you put it into a negative action, and you lose control that it becomes destructive. Most times, you only end up hurting yourself then."

She brushes a finger beneath one of the cuts.

"You kicked him," I remind her. "How's that different from me hitting him?"

She smiles up at me. "I didn't hurt myself because I didn't lose control."

I nod, finally understanding. Feeling like shit because I lost my temper in front of her, I whisper, "I'm sorry. I'm not such a nice person, after all."

Her smile doesn't lose any of its strength. "So far, you're the most caring person I've ever met. Even your laughter sounds kind."

I reach for her face and brush my thumb over her cheek. "Thanks, Lee. I really needed to hear that."

Chapter 9

Lee

Speechless, I can only stare at all the bags.

"I'll help you unpack everything," Lake says, and picking up the first bag, he begins to take clothes out, placing them on the bed.

I shake my head to get out of the stunned daze and step forward. "Wait." I take the bag from him and set it back down with the others. "What is all of this?"

"Just things you might need," he explains.

"When will I ever need all of this?" I shake my head again, still not able to believe Lake ordered so many clothes for me. "I can't accept all of this."

"Why not?" He turns away from the bed and faces me.

Looking up at him, I take in his kind brown eyes. This man has surprised me in so many ways. He just keeps giving, never asking for anything in return.

"How will I pay you back?" I ask.

He brings a hand to my arm, and the moment I feel the warmth from his palm on my skin, it makes a foreign sensation spin a delicate web in my stomach. Feeling self-conscious, I lower my eyes to his chest.

Lake lifts his other hand to my face, and when he places a finger beneath my chin, an overwhelming emotion shoots up from my stomach, slamming into my heart, which only makes it beat faster.

He nudges my face up, and as our eyes meet, he says, "It's a gift, Lee."

I swallow hard and whisper, "It's too much for a gift."

The corner of his mouth begins to pull up, and the movement catches my eye. Then he tilts his head, and an intense look, I haven't seen before settles on his face. It fills his eyes with such tenderness, it makes the emotion in my chest spread out, like the first rays at sunrise coming into view on the horizon.

Lake moves his hand from my chin down to my neck, and he keeps still for a moment, just looking into my eyes.

A slow smile forms around his lips, and brushing his fingers over my racing pulse, he pulls me closer with his other hand before wrapping his arms around me.

For a while, I stand still just breathing in his scent.

The man holding me so affectionately is going to become my husband.

The thought doesn't fill me with fear or panic any longer and realizing this, I bring my arms up and wrap them around his waist. Turning my head, I rest my cheek against his chest, while a relieved smile softly settles around my mouth.

I have been shown more kindness in the past two days than I've experienced in my entire life.

Lake tightens his arms around me and lowers his head until I feel his breath stirring my hair and fanning over my forehead.

"I know it's asking a lot, but will you allow me to take care of you?" His voice rumbles softly.

Squeezing my eyes shut, my heartbeat speeds up even more as I ask, "What will you expect of me in return?"

My question makes Lake pull back, and my heart shoots into my throat. Nervously my eyes dart to the bed and just seeing it has me forgetting to breathe.

"Hey," he whispers. Framing my face with his hands, he takes a step to the side, so I have to look at him and not the bed. "I don't expect anything from you that you're not willing to give freely."

"Jinjja?" The word just pops over my lips while I struggle to find the right English word.

Lake lets out a chuckle. "Yes, really." Then he jokes, "Thank God, I understand that one." Placing one arm around my shoulders, he moves until he's standing next to me, and then we both stare at all the bags.

"It's still too much," I say, pulling a worried face because I don't even know where I'm going to put it all.

"Okay, let's negotiate," he offers.

"One bag," I immediately say.

"Okay, we can take one away," he comments, and when I glance up at him with a frown forming on my forehead, he begins to chuckle. "At least keep half. It will make me feel better."

He's willing to compromise, which means I should do the same. I still have no idea what I'm going to do with everything, but I nod and bow my head slightly, "Thank you."

Then I hear movement and the rustling of more paper bags behind me, and glancing over my shoulder, I watch Mason carry more stuff into the room. "Where should I put this?"

My mouth drops open, and my head quickly turns to Lake, "There's more?"

He pulls a cute face and scrunching his shoulders up, he says, "Sorry?"

"Eomeo." I bring my hands to my cheeks and stare at him with huge eyes, "Gwiyeobda!"

"Holy shit," Mason mumbles next to us, and I quickly glance at him. He's staring at both Lake and me. "Buddy, I'm sorry to say this, but you're fucked."

"I just realized that," Lake says, then he takes hold of my arm. "Do that again."

"What?" I ask, not understanding what they're talking about.

"The huge eyes, excited thing you just did," Mason tries to explain.

"Like this?" I ask, and I bring my hands to my cheeks again and widen my eyes.

129

"Now, add the words."

I finally catch on to what Mason is talking about and decide to try something different. Keeping my hands against my cheeks, I furrow my brow and pout at Lake, pretending to look sad. "Oppa! Lee can't take all of this."

Lake rubs a hand over his face, and I get a glimpse of a huge smile as he turns slightly away from me. He places a hand over his heart and protests, "Shit, that's too cute."

He keeps sneaking peeks at me, so I up my level of cuteness. I place the tip of my forefinger on my bottom lip and turning my head from one side to the other, I go, "Humf, humf... Oppa, this is too much for Lee."

Lake just stares at me for a little while, and when he darts forward, I let out a squeak of surprise. Moving in behind me, he wraps an arm around the front of me and pulls me back until I'm practically locked to his chest. When I try to glance up at him from over my shoulder, he shakes his head and leaning down, he buries his face in my neck.

"No more," he chuckles, and I feel the sound vibrate through my back. "You're too cute for me to handle right now."

"Yep, like I said," Mason grumbles, "You're fucked."

"Who? Why?" Kingsley asks as she comes into the room, carrying a bag.

"I did this," I say, and when I lift my hands to my cheeks, Mason drops the bags, grabs Kingsley, and places a hand over her eyes. Lake rushes to take hold of my wrists and pin them to my chest.

"No way in hell am I letting you teach her that," Mason exclaims, and begins to drag her out of the room.

Kingsley laughs and tries to pull his hand away from her eyes. "I want to see."

Laughter bubbles over my lips as I watch Mason lift her off her feet and carry her out of the room, while arguing, "No, you're cute enough."

When I hear the door to the suite click shut, I slowly become aware of the fact that Lake has me pinned to his chest.

Lake

When we're alone, I can't make myself let go of Lee. Not yet.

It feels like I'm bursting with affection for this woman after all the cute faces she made. It makes me wish I could lock her in my heart and keep her there.

Earlier, when I placed my hand against her neck, I could feel her pulse racing. The moment made me realize Lee no longer sees me as a stranger.

She's already relaxed so much around the group and myself, and every time I get to learn something new about her, it makes my feelings for her grow.

Seeing the interest in her eyes when she looks at me fills me with relief and happiness. I've lived the past two years with the knowledge I would marry her. But now that I'm getting to see her smile, hear her laughter, and I'm able to touch her, it makes everything an overwhelming reality.

It feels like I'm watching my hopes and dreams come to life.

Even though she's not shying away from me anymore, I don't want to push her. Pressing a kiss to her shoulder, I reluctantly loosen my hold on her.

She doesn't dart forward, like she would've done yesterday, but instead turns around and smiles at me before she looks at all the bags, "Where do I even start?"

Grinning, I pick up the closest bag and tip it over on the bed. I pick up a black shirt and shake my head, throwing the fabric to the side. "I think we should separate all the dark colors and throw them out."

"Why?" she asks, picking up the black shirt and folding it neatly.

"Because light and colorful clothes will flatter you most," I explain, and begin to work my way through all the items until there's a neat heap of dark colors stacked on the right side of the bed. "I think that solves the problem,' I mumble.

Lee lets out a chuckle as she starts to place the stacks back into empty bags.

When I pick up the last shopping bag and spill the contents on the bed, Lee makes a squeaking sound and diving over the mattress, she covers the underwear with her body.

Scrambling to gather everything, she hurriedly shoves them back into a bag, then sits on the bed, hiding it behind her back with an embarrassed look on her face, mumbling, "I can do those myself."

With a mischievous grin on my face, I dash forward and grab the bag from behind her. "I don't mind helping."

"Ya!" she exclaims, shooting up from the bed and reaching for the bag. I lift it higher and chuckle when she tries to jump so she can get to it.

I'm having way too much fun teasing her.

Lee grabs hold of my shoulder and stretches as far as she can. When I lift it a little higher, she slumps back to her feet, letting go of my shoulder.

She takes a step back and slowly lifting her head, she gives me a shy look, and it instantly makes my heart melt. Then she asks in the most adorable voice, "Can I please have the bag."

My hand lets go before I've even processed all the damn cuteness she's throwing my way.

She darts forward and scooping it up, a wide smile spreads over her face.

"Oh, I see you're still fucked," Mason suddenly says behind me, "I'll come back later with the rest of the stuff."

Only then do I think to lower my hand back down from where it was still hanging in the air like a limp noodle. I take two steps back and glancing into the living room, I watch Mason push Falcon to the door.

"What?" Falcon whispers.

"Just go. I'll tell you outside," Mason whispers back, shoving him out of the suite. He begins to pull the door shut but then sees me. The ass lifts both his hands to his face, trying to imitate Lee, which has me letting out a bark of laughter and almost falling backward. I grab hold of the door jamb and quickly straighten up, so I don't land on my ass in front of Lee.

When I glance at her, there's no sign of the underwear bag, and she's already busy packing clothes into the closet.

Chapter 10

Lee

Lake and his friends are all in classes and feeling restless from not having anything to do, I walk down a path which looks like it might lead into the woods that are right behind the restaurant.

On top of all the clothes, Lake also gave me a phone. Preston showed me how to use it, and I got to speak to my mom an hour ago. She coughed a lot during the call, and when I asked her if she was getting sick, she brushed it off, telling me there was just something stuck in her throat.

I forgot to ask her what she's doing with all the free time now that she doesn't have to work anymore after Chairman Park gave her money.

I'm pulled out of my thoughts when someone calls, "Miss Park."

Glancing in the direction of the restaurant, I see the waiter who served us yesterday, gesturing for me to come in.

The moment I walk inside the airconditioned building, the waiter says, "It's already three pm. Chef Anand prepared your lunch at twelve."

"I'm sorry, I didn't know we had to eat at specified times."

The waiter chuckles and shaking his head, he says, "There's no specific time. Have a seat at this table. I'll tell Chef Anand you're here."

I pull out a chair, and when I glance around me, I notice other students watching me. A wave of self-consciousness ripples over me, and I quickly turn my eyes to the table in front of me.

Suddenly, Chef Anand says, "Finally!" He places a bowl in front of me, and another next to me, before he sits down.

"You're joining me?" I ask, a smile spreading over my face.

"I've missed the street food of Korea's markets," he admits.

"You've been to Korea?" I ask, my eyes widening with surprise.

"I lived there for five years while I studied traditional Korean cuisine."

I look down at the bowl of Tteokbokki, and smelling the familiar spices reminds me of home, making nostalgia settle heavy in my heart.

Eomma, I miss you so much.

I close my eyes and do my best to push the heartbreaking feelings down.

Glancing at Chef Anand, I first have to take a trembling breath before I can say, "Thank you."

"Jal meokgesseumnida," he says, then begins to eat.

"Jal meokgesseumnida," I repeat, and picking up my chopsticks, I take a bite. "Eomeo, sooooo good," I mumble around a mouthful of rice cakes, drenched in spicy sauce.

When my bowl is empty, and my heart and stomach is full, I say, "Jal meogeosseumnida."

Chef Anand pats the corners of his mouth with a napkin, then he looks at me with an appreciative smile. "It's such a pleasure preparing meals for someone who doesn't complain about everything. Mandu is on the menu for tomorrow."

I grin happily at him while we get up from our seats. I bow my head slightly, feeling nothing but gratitude toward him for lightening my burden by giving me a taste of home.

When I meet his eyes again, I ask, "Is there any work I can do? Maybe in the kitchen? I've worked in restaurants before." When he takes a moment to think, I quickly add, "I'll work for free. I would just really like something to do."

He gives me a stern look but then says, "You can begin by clearing this table."

I don't miss the smile spreading over his face as he turns around and walks back to the kitchen.

Feeling energized, I quickly gather the dishes and chopsticks and rush after Chef Anand.

Thirty minutes later, Chef Anand's voice booms through the kitchen, "Why are there no plates!"

I stop wiping the counter and glance over my shoulder at the pile of dishes. There's only one woman in front of the sink, and she looks exhausted.

I dart over to her and whisper, "Let me take over while you rest."

She lets out a tired sigh, and without saying anything, she walks out of the kitchen. I load all the dishes into the soapy water and begin to wash. Soon I fall into a routine of wash, rinse, and dry – and it makes a familiar calm settle over me.

Lake

After class, I try to call Lee so I can ask her to meet us for an early dinner. When the call goes to voicemail, I let out a chuckle. "I give her a phone, and she doesn't use it."

"Lee?" Falcon asks.

"Yes. You guys go ahead," I say, and when I walk toward the dorm, Layla and Kingsley come out of the lobby. "Did you see Lee upstairs?"

"No, she's not in her suite. We knocked a couple of times," Layla answers.

"Maybe she's already eating?" Kingsley asks.

Shrugging, I squeeze in between the girls and place an arm around each of their shoulders. "While we're walking there and I have a moment alone with you, I want to say thank you."

"For what?" Layla asks, looking a little confused.

"Crap, did we forget to do something?" Kingsley asks.

I let out a chuckle and shake my head. "Thanks for welcoming Lee with open arms. It means a lot to me."

Kingsley pulls away and punches me against the arm. "Ow, what's that for." I pretend it hurt by rubbing over the spot.

"I seriously thought we forgot to do something," she grumbles, but then a smile spreads over her face. "You really don't have to thank us, Lake. She's a part of the group."

I give her a grateful smile, and entering the restaurant, we head over to our usual table while I glance around for any sign of Lee.

Jeremy, our usual waiter, comes to the table and frowns when I don't sit down. "Mr. Cutler?"

"Everyone can order. I'm going to go look for Lee," I say, but before I can walk away, Jeremy says, "She's in the kitchen."

"What?" I ask, not sure I heard him right.

There's a flash of worry on his face when he repeats, "Miss Park is in the kitchen."

Frowning, I walk to the kitchen, and when I step inside and my eyes land on the girl by the sink, my feet come to a faltering stop. My lips part and I'm flooded with amazement as I watch her work.

Lee's hair is tied back, and there's a contented smile on her face. Her movements are hypnotic, and she works at a speed I never knew was humanly possible.

Seeing the real Park Lee-ann in her element will be imprinted on my heart and in my memory forever.

I thought Layla was special, but Lee... she's on another level.

A waiter places a stack of dishes on the counter, and Lee's smile grows as she calls out, "Thank you for the work."

She's extraordinary in ways I can't begin to describe. I know deep in my heart if I keep her at Trinity with me, the same thing will happen to her that

142

would've happened to me if I had joined CRC – she will only end up losing herself.

I can't let that happen.

There's a vibrancy about her that's been missing from my life. She's different from everything I've ever known.

She's the change I've been craving.

An emotion I've never felt before begins to bubble in my chest. It feels like a mixture of excitement and promise.

I want to experience her way of living, her island, and her people.

I want to view the world through Lee's eyes because I know it will the most awe-inspiring thing I will ever see.

When I sit down at the table, Falcon asks, "Did you find her?"

"Yes, she's in her element right now." Wanting to avoid further questions, I ask, "Did you guys place your orders?"

Mason nods. "Kingsley ordered a steak with chicken wings on the side for you."

I grin at Kingsley. "Thanks."

"Have you spoken to your father lately?" Falcon asks Layla.

"Yes, he's in Egypt now."

As Layla tells everyone about her father's latest travels, my eyes go to Mason and Falcon.

They're my brothers, and God knows, I love them so much, but… what will happen to our bond if I leave? Will we slowly drift apart?

Years from now, when I'm living the life I've always dreamt of, will it be at the cost of our brotherhood?

We always spoke about how Mason would run CRC with Julian, and Falcon would create a new company.

Both their lives are playing out exactly like we planned.

And me? I would marry Park Lee-ann.

We joked about how I could run a café somewhere in Europe, but it was only an idea we were throwing around.

I never thought the day would come where I would have to choose between who I love most and what I want most.

Falcon laughs at something Layla said, but then he glances at me, and when our eyes lock, his smile slowly fades from his face.

Our food comes, and the conversation stays light while we eat, but I catch Falcon glancing at me every couple of minutes.

When we're done eating, the waiter clears the plates away and brings us each a coffee.

I listen to my friends talk, and when we're the last students in the restaurant, Layla gets up but then stops when Falcon remains sitting. "Aren't we going to the dorm now? I'm sure they want to close."

Falcon shakes his head. "You and Kingsley can go ahead. I need to talk to Mason and Lake."

Once the girls have left, and we're still sitting at the table, the waiter comes to ask, "Is there anything else I can get you."

Falcon leans back in his chair, saying, "No, we're going. Thanks."

"Have a good evening, sir." I watch the waiter rush off toward the kitchen.

"We're leaving?" Mason asks. "Why didn't we go with the girls then?"

"We're going for a walk," Falcon answers. He rises to his feet and walks to the entrance without another word.

"I guess we're going for a walk," Mason mumbles as he gets up.

"This walk might just kill me," I whisper as I follow them out of the restaurant and down the path that runs through the woods up to the cliff.

A couple of minutes later, Mason grumbles from behind me, "Not that I'm complaining, but whose brilliant idea was it to hike through the woods at eleven fucking pm?"

"Think of it as a midnight stroll," Falcon chuckles from the front.

"Midnight stroll my ass." For a while, I only hear our breaths blending with the night sounds, then Mason asks, "How far is this fucking midnight stroll going to be?"

"Shut up and enjoy the damn night air," Falcon growls.

I smile as I walk in the middle, but then a thought crosses my mind, and it makes overwhelming sadness fill my heart.

When we graduate, Mason will start working, and he'll probably get a place of his own. There's a good chance Falcon will propose to Layla, and they'll build their own home.

And I won't see Falcon in front of me or feel Mason behind me anymore.

Chapter 11

Lake

When we reach the cliff, we stand and stare out over the lights scattered below.

"Remember the pact we made when we were turned eighteen?" Falcon asks, his voice nothing more than a murmur.

"Fuck work," Mason chuckles.

"Fuck family," Falcon says the second line.

I close my eyes and struggle to hold back the tears, as I whisper, "Fuck everything but us."

Mason kicks a rock off the cliff. "In three months, I'll start working."

"After graduating, I'm going to ask Layla to marry me." I smile through the sadness because I know with all my heart they will be happy together.

"Yeah?" Mason asks.

"Yeah," Falcon lets out a sigh. "It would be great if we could have our engagement party on the same day Clare gets locked behind bars."

"We're going to make it happen," Mason says with determination lacing his words. "I'm meeting with the DA on Monday. We'll find a way to have them both locked up."

Silence falls between us for a little while, and Falcon steps closer to me, placing his arm around my shoulders.

I glance up at the stars, but they all blur when Mason also moves closer, also wrapping his arm around my shoulders. It feels like I'm being torn in two and sucking in a trembling breath, the first tear rolls down my cheek.

"It doesn't mean the end of us," Falcon finally breaks the silence.

"There will never be an end to the bond we share," Mason confirms. "No matter where you are."

"I'd like to believe that," I whisper.

"What happened in the kitchen?" Falcon asks.

"I got a glimpse of the life I always dreamt off," I admit.

"Then, you should grab hold of it with both your hands and never let go," Falcom murmurs. "Even if it leads you down a different path from ours."

"You're thinking of going with Lee?" Mason asks.

I nod. "I want to experience her way of life."

"I can already see it," Mason chuckles. "Lee with her own restaurant, and Lake's eating all her profits."

"Fuck off," I laugh while elbowing him in the ribs.

Mason ruffles my hair, and when we turn our gazes back to the valley below, he says, "There's always the private jet."

"Worst case scenario, we'll plan our yearly vacations so we can spend it together," Falcon adds.

"Yeah," I whisper.

A couple of minutes later, Falcon says, "It's time for a new pact."

"We have to talk to each other at least once a day," Mason says.

"This coming from the future president of CRC. You're going to be balls deep in work," Falcon jokes.

"At least once a week," I murmur, "and not just a call. I want to see your faces."

"Definitely," Mason agrees.

"If one of us needs the other two, we have to be there for him," Mason says.

"Are you going to tell Kingsley to hold off on giving birth while you fly over to Lake?" Falcon asks, and it might sound funny, but the question just shines a huge spotlight on the reality we have to face.

Mason lets out a heavy sigh. "Fuck."

"Yeah," I whisper. "Fuck."

"Our friendship has lasted twenty-two years," Falcon murmurs. "We'll find a way to make it last another forty-four years."

"You planning on dying at sixty-six?" Mason asks, smacking Falcon upside the head.

"No, I plan on retiring, and we can all do that in the same place even if it's on a damn island."

"Now that's a good idea," I say, the corner of my mouth lifting into a smile.

"So, I have a question," Mason says.

"Yeah?"

"Aren't there typhoons on that side of the world?" he asks.

"Isn't that similar to a hurricane?" Falcon asks.

"Hell if I know, but I'm sure we'll be fine. Lee will know what to do."

"You better be fine. I don't want to switch on the TV and see your ass clinging to a tree on the eight O'clock news," Mason grumbles.

Lee

"We have to wash our faces twice. I like using this oil cleanser and then the green tea foam one," I say, my eyes on our reflections in the mirror.

Kingsley leans forward and grins at Layla, "See, I told you."

The guys left early this morning to go surf while Layla and Kingsley came over so I could show them the Korean ten-step skincare routine.

When we're done washing our faces, I pick up a bottle of toner and squirt some onto a cotton pad.

"I like these," Kingsley says, rubbing her fingers over one of the pads.

"Just dab the toner onto your skin," I say. "Don't wipe."

By the time we get to step six, which is when we put on facial masks, Layla falls back on the couch and shuts her eyes. "I'm napping for the next twenty minutes."

"Now you sound like Lake," Kingsley teases while she sits down on one of the pillows on the floor. "Actually, I haven't seen him napping much the last couple of days."

"It's because Lee's here," Layla mumbles. "The dude has to impress her."

"Lake likes sleeping?" I ask. I position another pillow close to Kingsley and sit down.

Kingsley gets a mischievous look on her face, and Layla sits up so fast, the mask almost falls off.

"Are you thinking what I'm thinking?" Kingsley asks her.

Layla nods then scoots down to the floor. "So, what would you like to know about Lake?"

A wide smile splits over my face wrinkling the mask, which makes Kingsley snort. She points a finger at me as she falls back, and more laughter explodes from her. Between gasping for air and laughing, she manages to say, "From eighteen… to eighty… in less than… a second."

When we stop laughing, I say, "Maybe I should ask him everything I want to know."

"Actually, now that I think about it," Kingsley murmurs as she glances at Layla, "Lake's practically perfect."

Layla nods. "He is."

"Then why the hell did I fall for Mason?" Kingsley asks, which has Layla cracking up.

Layla first catches her breath before she gives Kingsley an affectionate look. "Because your crazy plays well with his crazy."

"Oh yes," Kingsley grins a head-over-heels look on her face. "I fell in love with him when he said that."

I glance at Layla and ask, "When did you fall in love with Falcon?"

A beautiful smile spreads over her face, and then she whispers, "He kissed me like he was poisoned, and I was his only cure."

"U-wa," I murmur.

Kingsley looks at me and tilting her head she says, "I wonder what your and Lake's headline will be."

Lake

As my surfboard glides through the water, I feel the spray on my face.

This is exactly what we needed. Just the ocean and us while the sun is rising.

"Ahhh! Fuck!"

Yeah, and Mason crashing face-first into the water.

I smile as I ride the wave all the way to the end. It's moments like this when my heart's pounding in my chest and excitement's rushing through my veins, that I feel alive.

I get the same feeling when I look at Lee.

When we take a break, and we're sitting side by side on the beach, looking out over the ocean, I say, "After graduation, I want to take Lee to Korea so she can visit with her mother. I'll see what Jeju is like before I make any definite plans."

"That sounds like a good idea," Mason murmurs.

"Layla's dragging my ass all the way to Africa," Falcon says.

"Yeah? Are you going to see her dad?" I ask.

Falcon nods. "I have to admit I'm nervous as fuck."

"Are you going to ask him for his blessing?" Mason asks.

"That's why I'm nervous," Falcon answer, letting out an apprehensive chuckle.

"Mr. Shepard sounds like an amazing person, and he's Layla's father. I'm sure you'll get along," I say to encourage Falcon.

"What are your plans for this summer?" I ask Mason.

The corner of his mouth lifts. "I don't get a vacation, remember."

"Right," I grumble.

"I'll probably look for a place closer to CRC. Kingsley and I haven't talked about the future yet, but I think it will be fun looking at houses with her."

"You know what comes before all of that?" Falcon asks.

"What?" Mason glances over to Falcon, lifting an eyebrow.

"Exams," Falcon grumbles.

"Ugh… fuck." Mason falls back on the sand. "You think I can get Preston to write mine for me?"

"Talking about Preston," I say. "I haven't seen him since the two of you gave him a lesson on bra sizes."

Mason begins to chuckle. "He's probably hiding."

"I'll check on him when we get back to the Academy," Falcon says, and then he gets up. "Last surf, and then we head back."

Chapter 12

Lee

Sunday morning I get up before dawn and quickly get dressed in a pair of jeans and one of the t-shirts Lake bought for me.

Yesterday Lake asked me to be ready at five because he wants to spend some time with me.

I'm not going to lie, I feel very nervous when I walk out of my room. I'm tempted to try and call my mom again, but knowing it's late at night back home, I resist the urge. I tried calling her yesterday, but she didn't answer.

She was probably busy. I'll try again later.

When there's a knock at the door, I grab the keycard then go to open it quickly.

I smile when I see Lake. "Morning." Shutting the door, I get my sneakers from the cabinet and slip them on.

When I glance up at Lake, he says, "Morning. Are you ready?"

I nod, and when we walk down the hallway, the nervous feeling I have about spending time alone with Lake increases until it speeds up my heartbeat.

He presses the button for the elevator, and when the doors open, he waits for me to step inside before he follows. I move to the back and link my fingers in front of me while Lake leans against one of the side panels, and then he just stares at me.

"Do I have something on my face?" I ask, bringing a hand up to wipe around my mouth in case I missed some toothpaste.

Lake shakes his head, and his smile widens. "I'm just looking at you."

The corner of my mouth lifts, and I quickly glance down at my hands.

Reaching the bottom floor, Lake holds the door, and when I dart past him, he lets out a chuckle and whispers, "Cute."

Walking out of the building, we turn right and follow the path I wanted to explore the other day.

"Have you heard from your family?" Lake asks.

"No, and I don't expect to," I answer truthfully.

"I've been wondering about something," he says. "How did Jo Yoon-ha text me if she can't speak English?"

"She probably used one of those apps that translate languages for a person." I shrug, then add, "Or the secretary could've helped her."

It's still dark out, and as we walk toward a tunnel of trees, lamps light up the path ahead, and I stop walking so I can appreciate the beauty.

"So beautiful," Lake whispers.

"Yes," I smile and begin to walk again.

"I meant you," Lake says, and when my eyes dart up to his, he lets out a chuckle. "You're really beautiful."

"Thank you." Unable to keep the grin off my face, I quickly look down at my feet.

We walk in silence for a little while, and then the back of my hand accidentally brushes against Lake's, and it sends streaks of lightning zapping up my arm.

A smile forms around my mouth, and I press my lips together to try and hide it.

My heart begins to beat faster with every step we take, and I find myself glancing down at Lake's hand, hoping he would take hold of mine.

The moment begins to weave a magical spell around me, and it fills my chest with so many emotions; it feels like soon there won't be any space left for my heart.

And then… will I give it to him?

Before meeting him, my answer would've been no. Now, after seeing his kind eyes and hearing his happy laughter… and feeling his arms around me – yes.

When my chest begins to overflow with emotions for him, I'll give him my heart, and I'll pray that he'll never give it back to me.

My fingers begin to tingle as if an invisible current is passing in the slight space between us. Lake's hand brushes against mine for a split-second, and it's enough to make my breaths speed up.

I can't focus on anything but this man next to me. I'm aware of every step he takes, and the sound of his shoes crunching against the ground.

I wish I had the courage to reach out first.

161

I would slide my hand into his and curl my fingers around his palm, and I'd relish in the feel of his skin against mine.

Would he tighten his fingers around mine while chuckling?

I'd probably giggle, only embarrassing myself.

But it would be perfect. A flawless moment where a man I like holds my hand for the first time.

Lake

If my heart beats any harder, I'm sure she's going to hear it.

Twice our hands have touched, and twice I've let the opportunity pass me by.

Okay, if our hands touch for a third time, I'm totally going for it.

Shit, what if it doesn't happen?

How far is it still until we reach the cliff?

Another ten minutes?

Her hand touches mine, and it happens so damn fast I'm left wondering if it was all just my imagination.

Just take hold of her hand, Lake.

A couple of inches to the left, buddy.

Damn, why am I so nervous? It's not like this is my first time. I've hugged her already!

Fuck, we're at the cliff already?

I stop a couple of feet before the barrier, and I watch as Lee slowly inches closer, and then she tries to peek down. Having satisfied her curiosity, she takes a couple of steps back and then stares out into the distance.

"Do you have any friends back home?" I ask.

"Not like you have here," she answers. "Sometimes, I'd go out with my co-workers for dinner, and we'd sing karaoke afterward."

"You can sing?" I ask, surprise in my voice.

She lets out a burst of laughter and shakes her head. "No, but it's fun."

"What else do you do for fun?"

Lee thinks for a while, then answers, "I would sometimes go to the Ajjuma next door and help her make clay pots. Even though she always scolded me for not doing it right, I think she enjoyed my visits."

Wanting to know everything about her, I ask, "Did you want to study after school?"

She shakes her head. "I never thought of things like that."

"Then what did you want to become once you finished school?"

She looks up at me and frowns slightly. "What do you mean?"

Rephrasing my question, I ask, "Wasn't there a certain career you wanted to do? When you thought of your future, what were your dreams?"

"Before I was told I was going to marry you?"

I nod, and she first stares out over the valley where the first rays of the sun are starting to lighten the sky.

"I just wanted to work. I didn't care what kind of job it was, as long as I could pay the rent and make sure there was enough food." Lee's quiet for a moment, then she asks, "What are your dreams when you think of the future?"

I let out a silent chuckle and take a step closer to her. "I want to do something that will make me feel content at the end of the day. I've thought about opening a café or a restaurant, but it doesn't fill me with excitement."

"What do you mean by excitement?" she asks, tilting her head to the side as she focuses all her attention on me.

"Remember Friday night while you were washing dishes?" I ask. When she nods, I continue, "You had this smile of pure contentment on your face. It was as if every plate filled you with excitement, and you couldn't wait to clean it."

"Oh, but that's because I enjoy working. I would do anything as long as I can stay busy."

For a moment, I contemplate whether now is the right time to mention it but then figure what the hell. "Summer vacation starts at the end of May."

"You'll be finished with your studies then, right?" she asks.

I nod. "We could spend the summer on Jeju with your mom."

Her entire face transforms from relaxed to shocked to emotional in a couple of seconds. She slowly brings her hands up and covers her mouth while her eyes widen, and when they begin to shine, I just react instinctively and walk to her.

I wrap my arms around her and pull her to my chest. Pressing a kiss to her hair, I say, "I'm going to take you home."

"Jinjja?" she mumbles against my chest.

"Yes, really." She pulls her arms from between us, and when she wraps them around me, it only makes me hold her tighter.

Whenever Falcon held Layla or Mason hugged Kingsley, it looked like they were two puzzle pieces that fit perfectly. And it made me wonder what Lee and I would look like to others if we hugged.

Lee fits so perfectly against me that there's no doubt in my mind that people won't see two puzzle pieces, but just one solid piece.

I pull back a little and bring my one hand up to her cheek, and first tuck some hair behind her ear, before I place a finger under her chin, nudging her face up until she looks at me.

"For two years, I wondered what you would be like. I literally spent hours thinking about you and whether we would be able to make a marriage work between us."

She rests her hands on my sides, and it makes the corners of my mouth lift.

"I used to find myself hoping we would just like each other instantly. I figured it would make things easier. When we started with the video chats, I thought shit this girl is stunning, and as time went by, I got used to thinking of you as my fiancée."

I glance out over the distance for a couple of seconds before I bring my eyes back to her. This is something I have to tell her before shit goes sideways, and I don't get the chance again.

"And then I met you and… to say you were a dream come to life would be an understatement." I frame her face with both my hands and lock my eyes with hers. "Even if this deal between your father and CRC falls through, I still want to date you. I still want the chance to get to know everything about you."

Her tongue darts out, and she wets her lips, instantly drawing my eyes to her mouth.

I'm still staring like an idiot when she pulls away, and then she says, "When I got home and met my father for the first time, I was told I'd marry an American man. I had just turned sixteen, and didn't even have the time to think about boys." She gives me an apologetic look. "I didn't want to leave my home. I didn't want to marry you. After my mother had me, my father got a mistress, and she gave him the son he wanted. I didn't want the same life for myself."

Every word I hear feels like it's strangling my heart.

Lee turns away from me and faces the sunrise. "I didn't want to marry you, only to be discarded after I gave birth to the next heir. I spent two years trying to think of ways I could make you hate me so you would break off the engagement."

I close my eyes because it hurts to hear the truth, but I have to listen because this is Lee's story and how she feels matters.

"Then... I met you." She pauses for a little while before she continues, "You have the kindest eyes. That was my first thought when I saw you."

I hear her move and opening my eyes, I see her coming closer to me. She looks down, and for a moment, she hesitates before she reaches out and takes hold of my hand. Bringing our hands up between us, she brushes her thumb over the back of mine. "I wondered whether your hands would be cruel or kind."

Too quickly, she lets go of my hand, and I have to hold myself back, so I don't reach for her again.

"Walking around campus, I've seen how other guys treat girls. I even kicked one of them." She lets out a chuckle. Lifting her eyes to mine, the smile stays around her lips. "You've respected my culture and me. You took me in, and you haven't once treated me like I was a stranger from another country. Your friends accepted me without asking any questions. I learned that even when you get angry, and you make a mistake, you apologize. Everything changed the moment we came here."

She takes a deep breath, and then her features soften, and I see emotions in her eyes, she hasn't allowed me to see up until now.

My heartbeat speeds up again, and a smile begins to pull at the corners of my mouth.

"I no longer want to make you hate me, Lake. I now want to know what it would be like to hold the hand of the man I like for the first time."

I take a step closer to her, not breaking eye contact. Slowly, I move my hand forward until it brushes against hers, and then I pull back an inch. The smile on my face stretches when her lips part, and she begins to breathe a little faster.

The same nervousness from earlier begins to drift back to me, but now there's a sense of excitement chasing its heels.

And this time when I move my hand, and it brushes against hers, I feel her fingers move as if they're searching for mine. I slide my palm over hers and link our fingers, making Lee glance down with the most beautiful smile on her face.

I brush my thumb over her soft skin, and ask, "Is it what you hoped it would be?"

"Much more," she whispers. She brings her eyes back to mine. "It's so much more."

Chapter 13

Lee

Glancing up at Lake, I allow myself to look at him with new eyes, and behind his kind gaze, I see a man who has the courage to protect those he cares for. There's integrity, and it makes him stand out head and shoulders above any other man.

And with the heart of a young girl who has never dared to dream, I take in his western features, which are so very different from my own. Lifting my hand up to his face, I brush my fingers along his temple. Even though his eyes hold a world of warmth, his eyebrows are sharp, and it gives me the impression he sees everything, even the things I try to hide.

My fingers trail down to the stubble on his jaw, and for the first time, I touch bristles, and I'm surprised by how soft they are.

I let my hand move down his neck, and then I stop for a moment because there's a fluttering in my stomach, and it makes me take deeper breaths. Lowering my palm to the middle of his chest, I close my eyes, and I feel the strong energy coming from his aura.

"You're like a lotus flower, pure and patient. You have love and compassion for all things," I whisper before I open my eyes, and I pull my hand back.

When I meet his eyes again, there's wonder shining from them, and then he whispers, "I don't know why they call it falling in love. It doesn't feel like I'm falling at all. It feels like I've finally found the other half of me, and every new discovery we make about each other brings us closer to being one."

Lake's fingers let go of mine, and then he lifts his hand to my face. His touch is soft as he rests his palm against my cheek, and the affection on his face makes my heartbeat feel like the swift fluttering of a hummingbird's wings.

"I want to kiss you." His voice is a low murmur, forming a bubble around us.

Anticipation trickles through me, and as he begins to lean down, my fingers curl into fists, so I'll keep still. He lifts his other hand to my neck, and his smile becomes gentle, softening his features with tenderness.

When I feel his breath fan over my face, my hands begin to tremble from the intense emotions it stirs inside of me. I close my eyes, and my breaths come faster over my lips until I feel the softness of his mouth press against mine – and I forget to breathe as the fluttering in my heart turns into humming.

Lake closes the small gap between our bodies, and he presses his chest against mine while tilting his head. His lips slowly open, and they caress mine in such an intimate way, it fills me with wonder that two people can create a moment that's so overwhelmingly intense with just their mouths.

Unfisting my hands, I bring them to his sides, and my fingers curl into the fabric of his shirt.

When Lake's mouth presses harder against mine, exhilaration flows from my stomach before it pours into my heart, and when it trickles over my skin, I begin to imitate the movements of his lips, learning what it means to share a kiss.

While the sun grows stronger over the horizon, I find myself getting lost in Lake as he gives me an experience I never knew existed.

He has shown me any bridge can be crossed, and it makes me realize how lucky I am.

I must've done something really good in a past life to have received such a generous gift as Lake Cutler in this life.

Lake

I feel her pulse racing under my palm, and it matches the beat of my heart while I breathe in her soft scent.

Feeling her reaction to my body pressing against hers while my mouth memorizes the curve of her lips, makes it so damn hard to not deepen the kiss.

It takes all of my strength to lift my head, especially when her breaths explode over my lips. When my eyes drift open, and I see the same intensity I feel on her face, I have to let go of her and take a step back, so I don't lose control and just give in to my need for more.

Lee's still caught in the moment, her hands suspended in the air where she was holding onto my sides, her chest rising and falling with every breath that rushes over her parted lips.

And I can only stare because I've never been more mesmerized in my life than I am from seeing how captivated she is by me kissing her.

I watch her come back from wherever the kiss took her. Opening her eyes, her arms fall to her sides, and her breaths begin to return to normal, while the blush in her cheeks deepens.

When she lowers her gaze to the ground, I move forward, closing the small distance between us, and I reach for her hand, lacing our fingers. I lift my other hand to the back of her neck and rest my cheek on the top of her head as I hug her, whispering, "Thank you."

Lee presses her cheek to my chest and nods. Raising her hand, she flattens her palm over my chest, and we stand like this for a long while, just staring out at the valley.

Lee

We follow the path back to the campus, and it feels like everything looks brighter. Even the leaves on the trees seem to be a deeper shade of green.

Every couple of minutes, I glance down at Lake's hand, holding mine tightly. But when we pass by the restaurant, and I see all the people, I try to pull my hand free.

Lake doesn't let go, and giving me a reassuring smile, he says, "Here it's normal to hold hands in public. People won't even notice."

Right, they don't frown on public displays of affection like people do back home.

I glance around me just to make sure we're not offending anyone when I see Lake's friends walking across the lawn toward the buildings where the classrooms are.

"There's Layla, Kingsley, and Preston," I say.

Preston looks in our direction, and he notices Lake is holding my hand. To get Layla's attention, he nudges her so hard she stumbles into Kingsley, who falls onto the grass, and it makes laughter burst from Lake.

Preston looks horrified by what happened, and he tries to help Kingsley up, but she only yanks him down, which has Layla sitting down on the grass because she's laughing so hard.

Lake has to stop walking, and grabs hold of his stomach as he hunches over with laughter, and the sound is so magical it makes me chuckle.

I pull my hand free from Lake's and pat him on the back while he struggles to breathe. "And you said it's normal," I say wryly. "People won't notice." I point to his friends. "We caused an accident."

Lake sinks to his knees, and he covers his face with his hand as tears of laughter spill over his cheeks.

I glance around us, and I notice more students laughing. We caused a happy accident, and it fills me with joy.

Lake finally manages to catch his breath, and I help him to his feet. Reaching up, I wipe a tear from his cheek.

Suddenly he takes hold of my face, and he presses a hard kiss to my mouth. I'm frozen with surprise, and before I can even catch up to what's happening, he lets go of me, saying, "You make me so happy."

"Does this mean we get a new mom?" Mason suddenly asks.

My head turns so fast in the direction of his voice, I almost sprain it.

Falcon and Mason walk toward us, and they both have huge grins on their faces.

"I forgot to tell you," Lake mumbles. "Because I'm the mature one –"

Mason lets out a bark of laughter. "Mature my ass."

He takes a patient breath, then continues, "It sometimes feels like I have five kids instead of friends."

"Oh, so that would make me the mother?" I ask.

Lake nods, and with a solemn face, he says, "I'm sorry I didn't tell you. Being a single father makes dating almost impossible, and I didn't want you knowing before... uhm... before..."

"Before I fell in love with you?" I help him find the words.

The solemn look is quickly replaced with one of hope as Lake whispers, "Did you?"

Reaching for his hand, I wrap my fingers around his, and I smile up at him. "Yes."

"Oh my God, that's the most romantic thing I've ever seen," a random girl says, and I step closer to Lake when she wipes a tear from under her eye.

When students begin to cheer and clap hands, I take another two steps to the right until I'm behind Lake, and I can hide my burning face against his back.

Lake

Knowing this must be embarrassing for Lee, I pull her from behind me and placing my arm around her shoulders, I begin to walk to the dorm.

I shoot Mason and Falcon a glare and mumble, "Thanks for that guys," as I pass by them.

A couple of steps further, Mason yells at the top of his lungs, "There's already five of us. Don't go making more babies."

"Eomeo," Lee squeaks. Lifting my other hand in the air, I give Mason the middle finger while I try not to laugh, but when I hear the guys cracking up behind me, I almost snort as the laughter escapes over my lips.

179

"Aww… this is such a proud moment for the family," Kingsley says to our left, and instead of me holding Lee, she has to place an arm around my back to keep me from sinking to the floor.

We somehow make it inside the building, and once we're in the elevator, I manage to catch my breath enough to calm down.

When I look at Lee, and I see her covering her cheeks with her hands, I step closer.

"It feels like my cheeks are on fire," she admits.

"Yeah?" I nudge her hands away and frame her face with mine. "How's that?"

"U-wa, so much better," she sighs, her eyes closing for a moment.

When the elevator opens, I steal a quick kiss and then dart away from her so I can catch the doors before they begin to close again.

"Now they're hot again," she mumbles under her breath as she walks past me and down the hallway.

When we step into her suite, I shut the door behind me. I notice her glance around as I sit down on the couch.

"Are you looking for something?"

She shakes her head, then sits down on one of the cushions, which makes me move down to the floor as well.

"I don't have anything to offer you to drink," she says. "It feels rude."

Unable to stop touching her, I reach over and brush some hair behind her ear. "Don't worry about it. I'm not thirsty."

There's a moment's silence, then I say, "How about we ask questions. That way, we get to know each other a bit better."

She nods, and a grin forms around her mouth. "You start."

I sit back against the couch, and drinking in her delicate features, I ask, "Which do you like most, mountains or the ocean?"

"Can't I answer both?" She scrunches her nose. "Jeju has both. We have a volcano in the middle of the island, and it has a big lake in the dome."

"Volcano?" It's the only word that sticks. "Like an actual active volcano that spews fire and stuff?"

She begins to laugh and shaking her head, she replies, "It hasn't erupted in thousands of years."

Letting out a sigh of relief, I mumble, "That's good to hear."

"Which do you like most?"

"Not a volcano, that's for sure," I joke. "I love the ocean. I can spend the whole day out there surfing."

"What's it like?"

I smile because my plan worked much better than I thought it would. Lee relaxes, and crossing her legs, she places her elbows on her knees and rests her face in her palms.

I straighten my legs to the side and cross them at the ankles while I try to think of the best way to explain surfing to her. "When you paddle out past the waves, and you sit on your board watching the sun come up over the water," I pause as I let the calm feeling wash over me, "It's so peaceful. Nothing but you and the ocean. It's a humbling experience."

Lee tilts her head, her eyes focused on me. "What makes it humbling for you?"

"Out there… it feels like the ocean accepts me even though I'm nothing in comparison to its power."

And I get the same feeling with you.

Chapter 14

Lee

Monday I keep watching the time, and the second it's twelve O'clock, I press dial on the phone.

Worry builds in my stomach, and I begin to chew on my thumbnail when the phone just keeps ringing.

Eomma, why aren't you answering?

I try again and again.

Eomma.

Fear slithers through me, and it coils around my heart, squeezing until it's weakened me, and a tear spills over my cheek.

I press dial again, and with every ring, my fear grows stronger.

Suddenly the ringing stops, and my breath hitches when I hear, "Yeoboseyo?"

At first, I'm so relieved I can't get a word out.

"Yeoboseyo?"

But then I recognize the voice of the Ajjuma next door, and it makes the fear give way to dread.

"Park Lee-ann?"

Hearing the urgency in her voice, I close my eyes, and I begin to pray a hopeless prayer.

"Yeoboseyo?"

"Ajjuma," I whisper, not prepared for what she will tell me.

Lake

Mason, Falcon, and I met with my father and his contact at the DA's office. Mason handed over all the evidence, and the DA said he'd do his best to get Serena the harshest sentence.

Now we have to wait for them to open the case against her, and once the court date is set, we'll have a front-row seat.

As we drive back to the Academy, my phone starts to ring. Seeing it's Kingsley, I frown. "Mason, is your phone switched off?"

"No, why?"

"Then why is Kingsley calling me?" I swipe up. "Hey, what's up?"

"You need to come back now." Kingsley's voice is so tight with worry, it makes me sit upright in a second.

"What's wrong?"

"It's Lee," she gasps.

"What happened to Lee?" I somehow manage to ask past the fear gripping my throat.

"Layla ran to the office to get a spare keycard because Lee won't open the door. She –" Kingsley pauses, and when I hear her sob, ice pours through my veins. "Oh God, she's breaking my heart. Get back here! I don't know what to do."

Falcon must've been watching my face because he says, "Mace, as fast as you can. Fuck speed limits."

Even though it only takes Mason ten minutes, it feels like I've aged years by the time he comes to a screeching halt in front of the dorm. I'm out of the car and running into the building as fast as I can. I take two stairs up at a time, and my breaths rush over my lips as I bust into the hallway on Lee's floor.

When I hear Lee's cry, it feels as if something reaches into my chest and rips my heart out.

I rush into her suite and come to a stumbling halt as my eyes land on her. Seeing her kneeling and clenching the phone to her chest while her entire being is torn with grief makes a physical pain spread through my chest.

Snapping out of the moment, I rush forward, and Kingsley moves away so I can drop to my knees next to Lee.

I try to frame her face with my hands, but she wildly yanks it away from me, and the cry that tears through her brings tears to my eyes.

"Andwae," she whimpers, and knowing I have to do something, I shift until I'm in front of her.

This time I use more force when I grab hold of her, and while everything in me just wants to comfort her, I snap harshly, "Look at me, Lee. You have to tell me what happened. I can't help if I don't know what's wrong. Tell me what happened."

Her eyes look feverish when they finally meet mine. "Tell me what happened," I repeat again.

"My mom," she gasps, and it rips a piece of my soul out when I watch another wave of grief takes her under.

"What can we do?" Falcon asks.

"I need to get her home. I need the jet," I answer, not taking my eyes away from her face.

"I'll call Stephanie," Mason says.

I try to wipe her tears away, but they keep falling, and I hate how powerless I feel at this moment, not being able to take her pain away.

Layla comes running into the room with the nurse right behind her, and I reluctantly move to the side so the nurse can take over.

"Miss Shepard says you got some bad news," the nurse says in a caring voice. "I'm going to give you something to help you calm down after I've checked your vitals, okay?"

Kingsley shuffles closer to me and wrapping her arms around my neck, she hugs me. Knowing Mason is busy because of me, I place my arm around Kingsley and comfort her while the nurse tends to Lee.

"Come, Kingsley," Layla whispers and taking hold of her arm, Layla pulls Kingsley away from me.

After the nurse checks Lee's vitals, she gives her a tablet to put under her tongue. Eventually, Lee stills as if someone flipped a switch, and she just blankly stares at nothing. It's even more heartbreaking to see than when she was crying.

The nurse doesn't seem to be worried. "Keep a close eye on her. If she gets worse, call me or take her to the hospital."

"Okay," I answer. The moment the nurse leaves, I move back to Lee and wrapping my arms around her, I pull her to my chest.

Falcon crouches next to me and whispers in my ear, "Mace says we can take off in three hours. I'll ask Layla to pack for the girls, and I'll take care of ours."

I nod, turning my head to Falcon, and I take a couple of deep breaths while I get the strength I'll need for the next couple of days just from looking at him.

The past eighteen hours have been absolute hell, but when we walk out of the airport at Jeju, and I see the flash of relief on Lee's face, I know I would do it again for her.

Holding Lee's hand, I turn to the group. "Why don't you go get us settled in the hotel. I'll call you when I know more."

"Okay," Falcon answers. "Are you sure you don't want one of us to come with you?"

"I'm sure. You're all tired as well. I'll call the second I find out anything."

Falcon places a hand on my shoulder and gives it a squeeze, then whispers, "Good luck, buddy."

"Thanks." I give him a smile before I turn back to Lee. "Can you call us a cab?"

Nodding, she darts forward, and I have to move to keep up with her. She finds one, and I have my doubts about the car, but Lee gives me no choice when she climbs into the back.

She gives the driver the address of the hospital her mother is in... I think, before she hurriedly says, "Ppalli! Ppalli!" and then she softly adds, "Jebal."

After a couple of minutes, I'm no longer holding Lee's hand to offer her support, but holding on for dear life as the cab weaves in and out of lanes.

By the time we stop in front of the hospital, I'm feeling nauseous. Taking out my wallet, I hand it to Lee so she can pay the driver from the Korean won notes I got at the airport.

She hands it back to me, and I first get out of the cab before I tuck it back in my pocket. The second Lee is out of the cab, she runs.

I'm right behind her as we hurry through the entrance, and then I hear, "Yeogi! Park Lee-ann, Yeogi! Ppalli!"

"Ajjuma," Lee calls out as she rushes over to the older woman, and after that, I have no idea what they're saying.

We follow the older woman, and I'm guessing she's explaining to Lee what happened to her mother. It feels like I'm moving through a beehive with all the different hallways we walk down and the foreign language filling the air.

When we stop outside a room, Lee takes a couple of deep breaths, and she pats her cheeks. She somehow finds the strength to smile before she walks into the room.

The older woman inclines her head a couple of times in my direction, and I make sure to bow lower than her before I glance inside the room. There are four beds, but only two have curtains pulled around them.

I walk toward the corner where Lee just stands staring at the bed, and when I get closer, I see her mother where's she's on life support.

Lee slowly moves closer, and then she reaches out with a trembling hand and brushes her fingers lightly over her mother's forehead. "Eomma?"

I step closer to the wall and lean my shoulder against it, giving Lee the time she needs. It looks like a million words flow from Lee to her unconscious mother, and I can only imagine how sad they must be.

I don't know how much time has passed when a doctor comes in, followed by two nurses. When the doctor starts talking to Lee, I wish I brought Preston along so he could translate.

"Andwae," Lee murmurs, shaking her head.

When a pleading look settles on her face, I walk closer. I place my hand on her lower back and ask, "What are they saying?"

Lee looks up at me with such hopelessness she doesn't have to say the words.

"H-her lung collapsed." She takes a deep breath, and a tear rolls over her cheek. Reaching up, I wipe it away while I wrap my arm around her. "They say she won't wake up and…" her breathing hitches, and she whispers, "Andwae."

The doctor moves toward the machines, which has Lee crying, "Jebal! Jebal!"

She asks something of them to which they seem to agree, and I wait for them to leave before I look at Lee. Before I can ask a question, she says, "They… they gave me time to say goodbye."

Fuck.

I press a kiss to the side of her head and say, "I'm just moving to the other side of the curtain so you'll have privacy. If you need me, just call."

She nods, and as I walk a couple of steps away, I watch her move right to the side of the bed, and then her face crumbles. I bring both my hands up, covering my mouth as my eyes begin to burn.

"Eomma," she whispers. "Je...bal."

I hear her start to cry, and I have to close my eyes as tears flood them. Her hitching breaths and sobs cut through me, and it's the most painful thing I've ever felt.

Knowing the person you care for is hurting, and there's nothing you can do. It's indescribable torture.

"Salanghaeyo," she whispers, "Salang…hae…yo."

I don't know how long I stand here listening to her talk to her mother, but when the doctor and nurses come back, my heart drops to my stomach. I dart around the curtain, which has Lee's head snapping up, and she immediately begins to cry harder.

I wrap my arms around her and hold her tightly as they say something to her, which has her screaming into my chest.

Her breaths explode harshly over her lips, and she pulls back, taking a step toward her mother, but then she freezes as her eyes land on something by the door.

I turn my head, and when I see Mr. Park standing there, watching his daughter grieve for her mother with no expression on his face, it's as if something snaps inside of me.

Before I can react, Lee grabs hold of my hand. She turns her back to Mr. Park and whispers, "The law is not on our side here." She looks up at me with pleading eyes. "I'm eighteen. I cannot leave Korea without his consent."

Fuck, that's a big problem.

Not that we have time to discuss this right now, I still ask, "So if I cancel the contract with him before we get married, you have to come back to Korea?"

She nods and glances over her shoulder, which has me looking as well. Mr. Park comes toward us, and he doesn't even bother to look at Lee.

Fuck, this is going to be hard. All I want to do is hit him until he's lying half-dead in one of these beds.

"Mr. Cutler, I didn't expect to see you here," he says.

I take a deep breath, and when Lee tightens her hold on my hand, I force a smile to my lips. "I should've notified you, Chairman Park. My apologies."

I glance at Lee. *For you, I'll give an Oscar-worthy performance today.*

The doctor presses a button on one of the machines, which has Lee's head snapping back to her mother.

"I've signed for them to switch off the machines," Mr. Park says.

God, give me strength.

"I thought you were divorced?"

"Only separated."

Fuck.

"Can we please have ten minutes so Lee can finish her farewell?"

"Of course." He snaps something at the doctor, who leaves with the nurses.

"Thank you." I turn to Lee and giving her hand a squeeze, I say, "I'll wait outside with Chairman Park."

She nods, and I can see it's taking all her strength to keep her tears back in front of him.

Reluctantly, I let go of her hand, and I gesture for Mr. Park to walk first. As I leave Lee to say her final goodbye, my mind begins to race to find a legal loophole so I can keep Lee with me and tell this man to shove his investment up his ass.

Once we're out in the hallway, I glance at the older woman who's been waiting outside all this time, and I hope she understands when I gesture toward the inside of the room. She bows her head a couple of times, giving Mr. Park a wide berth as she rushes inside.

The corner of his mouth pulls up in a smirk as he says, "I was told you will only graduate in May."

"Yes, sir." *If I graduate at this rate.*

"That's a pity. I was hoping we could speed up the deal. I have other business to take care of."

"You want us to get married sooner?" I ask, thinking there might actually be a light at the end of this tunnel.

"Yes, if your father and Chairman Reyes agree, of course."

"I'm sure they will," I answer, knowing they will back me.

"Good. Well, my job here is done. Let me know when the date is set for the ceremony so we can sign the contract."

"Will do."

He looks at me as if he's weighing my words before he turns to leave. I watch him talk to the doctor, and I know I can't buy Lee any more time.

I rush back into the room and walking around the bed, I take hold of her shoulders and whisper, "Hug your mom. Tell her you love her."

Her body begins to shake uncontrollably with silent sobs as she leans over her mother and hugging her she whispers, "Salanghaeyo, Eomma… salanghaeyo."

The moment the doctor walks into the room. I lean over Lee, and taking hold of her, I pull her away from the bed.

She lets out a heartbreaking scream, which has me placing a hand under her knees and lifting her to my chest. I hold her close as I walk out of the room, not wanting her to see the moment they switch off the life support.

Lee wraps her arms around my neck and buries her face against me as she weeps. I keep walking until I finally find the exit and seeing a park across the street, I head toward it.

I sit down on the first bench I see, and keeping hold of Lee with my left arm, I dig my phone out with my right.

I dial Falcon's number and close my eyes against the pain shredding my heart.

197

"Where are you?" Falcon answers, sounding worried.

"Outside the hospital. Her mother passed away. I'm not coming to the hotel tonight. I'm taking her to her house so she can grief in privacy."

"Just keep in touch. I don't like not knowing where you are in a foreign country."

I nod even though he can't see me. "I'll text you the address once I have it." I let out a sigh, then add, "Be careful. Mr. Park knows we're here. I'll bring you up to speed with everything when I see you tomorrow."

"Just take care of yourself. Please, Lake," Falcon says, an urgency in his voice I haven't heard before.

"I will. You and Mace are the first I'll phone if I need help," I remind him.

"I know it's hard right now and hate not being there with you. Remember, we love you. We're here," Falcon says, and it makes it so damn hard to hold back the tears.

I clear my throat, before I reply, "Love you too."

I cut the call and shove the phone back in my pocket, and then I just hold Lee for a moment. Pressing a kiss to her hair, I whisper, "I'm sorry. I'm so fucking sorry."

Her breaths keep hitching as if she can't take a full one, and I wrap my arms tighter around her.

I'll never let anything hurt you like this again.

Chapter 15

Lake

Once Lee is a bit calmer, I lean my head closer to her, and ask, "Can you get us to your house, or should we go to the hotel?"

She pulls slightly away from me, and with a look of uncertainty, she glances around us.

Thankfully the older woman who I think is Lee's neighbor comes rushing across the street.

Not knowing what else to do, I bring up an app Lee showed me and speaking into the microphone, I say, "Take us home."

It translates my words, and when the woman nods, I feel relief wash over me.

"Gomapsseumnida," I thank her to which she inclines her head. I pick Lee up and follow the woman. When it looks like she plans to walk for a while, I try to remember what Lee called a cab. "Ah… Taxshi," I try to pronounce it.

"Ne, taegsi," she says with a smile, and I'm about to start thanking the heavens when she flags one down.

The lady opens the door for me so I can place Lee on the backseat. I gesture for her to sit in front while I jog around the back and get in. Placing an arm around Lee, I pull her to me. I take hold of her chin and lifting her face, I begin to worry when I see the blank expression. Even her breaths are slower than usual.

I press her head to my shoulder and place a kiss on her forehead. "I've got you. You're not alone." I try to think what else I can say to her to comfort her, but there's nothing. All I can do is assure her I'll be with her every step of the way. "Take all the time you need to grieve. I'm not going anywhere, so just lean on me."

When the cab stops, I really have no idea where we are. I get out and go to Lee's side and opening the door, I begin to slide my arms under her when she says, "I'll walk."

I'm surprised to hear her voice but so damn thankful as well. I pull back and help her get out.

Lee's neighbor quickly takes hold of Lee's arm, and after we've been walking for quite some time and we turn down another narrow alley, I begin to wonder if we're not going around in circles.

Damn, I lost count after the fifth or seventh alley.

We turn a corner, and then I mutter, "Of course there will be stairs."

Not just ten. They're narrow, and there are a lot.

Halfway up, I'm thinking I should really up my workout routine because I'm feeling the strain. I glance at Lee and her neighbor, and when they don't look affected at all, I take a deep breath and suck it up. If they can do this, then so can I.

When it looks like we've reached a dead-end, the woman points up while saying something to Lee.

Lee bows her head, and then she slips down the narrowest alley I've ever seen, but it's only a short distance before it opens up into a broader path. Lee makes a sharp left, and then we're going up more steps. When we reach a rooftop, I tilt my head and frown.

Not saying anything, I follow Lee to a door, and when she kicks off her shoes, I do the same. She opens the door, which I notice wasn't locked. I take one step inside, and then I stop because I'm struggling to believe what I'm seeing.

"This is home?" I ask.

Lee nods as she pours two glasses of water. She brings me one while she takes a couple of sips of her own. Taking the glass from her, I move deeper into the room. It only takes me four steps, and then I'm standing in the middle of what seems to be the only room.

There are so many questions I want to ask her, but they will all have to wait until she's in a better frame of mind.

Lee opens a door, and I catch a glimpse of a tiny bathroom before she shuts the door behind her.

Park Je-ha is a wealthy man. How could he let his wife and daughter live in a place like this?

How the hell did Lee survive for eighteen years, living like this, and still turn out to be the most extraordinary person I've ever met?

Lee

I've never felt ashamed of my home because… it was home. It was the room I shared with my mother.

Every night we would lay out our blankets, and before we would fall asleep, we'd talk about everything we had to do the following day.

Mom would always wait for me to fall asleep first. For eighteen years, her face was the last thing I saw at night, and the first thing when I opened my eyes again.

Now I'll never see her face again.

I've been to funerals before but never to one of someone I loved. I didn't understand why people would weep so uncontrollably… until today.

Tears burn my eyes, and I close them.

Eomma.

How could you leave me behind?

Kneeling down on the floor, I rest my head against the wall.

What am I supposed to do while my mother moves on to her next life? If I'm lucky enough to be reincarnated in the same life as her again, how will I find her?

Will she recognize me?

Eomma.

Even in this time of mourning, I know I can't be rude, and it forces me back to my feet. I wash my face and hands before I leave the bathroom.

The room is empty, and I walk to the door. Looking outside, I see Lake standing to the left. His arms are crossed over his chest as he stares at all the buildings.

I go back inside, and seeing the rice cooker, I walk over to it. Kneeling down next to it, I open the lid, and I see a scoop of rice still left at the bottom.

And it's as if the sight of it breaks something in me.

I grab hold of the rice cooker, and I begin to slam it against the floor.

Sucking in a breath of air, a strangled sound squeezes from my throat. It hurts, and when another one forces it's way up, I grab hold of my neck. Hunching over, I let out a silent scream as the finality of death cloaks me in black.

I begin to rock myself back and forth, and when I finally manage a full breath, I let out a devastated cry.

Eomma!

Come back.

Please. Please.

Don't leave me here alone.

205

Please.

Lake's arm comes around my waist from behind, and he pulls me back against his chest. He wraps his other arm over both of mine, and I drop the rice cooker as he locks me to his chest.

"I've got you," he murmurs as sobs rob me of my breath. "I'm here, Lee. I'm not going anywhere."

I've only really known him a week, and in the dark night of my soul, he's become my lighthouse.

Lake

I wouldn't wish the last four days of my life on my worst enemy.

No wait, that's a lie.

There's one person, and I wish I could make him suffer a million times more for what he's done to Lee.

After the cremation and ceremony, which mainly consisted of Lee crying in a room while people ate out in a small hall, Lee wanted to come to the temple to pay her last respects to her mother.

I watch Lee kneel in front of an altar that has a photo of her mother on it, and then she bows to the floor before she gets back up. She does it two more times then she rises to her feet.

I move forward, and I light an incense stick before I go stand slightly to the left of Lee. And for the first time in my life, I get down on my knees. As I bow, I promise to honor, protect, and to love her daughter.

I climb to my feet and look at the picture of Lee's mother. She looks like she was a proud woman.

When Lee is ready, I take her hand, and we walk out of the temple. We put on our shoes before we climb down the steps to where the group is waiting by the van.

Mason got tired of cabs and rented a van with a chauffeur. If I had the energy, I would've laughed.

The chauffeur drives us to the airport, and only when the jet begins to gain speed, and the wheels lift off the runway, do I let out a sigh of relief that I managed to get Lee out of the country without any further problems from Mr. Park.

I glance around the cabin, and the corner of my mouth lifts when I see Kingsley lying with her legs draped over Mason's lap.

Mason glances up, and he catches my eyes.

Where one goes, the other two follows.

I move my eyes to Falcon and see how he presses a kiss to Layla's temple. When he pulls back, his eyes lock with mine over the top of her head.

This is how we'll live our future. Always together.

I tighten my grip on Lee's hand, and she turns her body toward me, pulling her legs up onto the seat. Reaching over to her, I place my hand behind her head, and when I lean in to kiss her forehead, she lifts her face, and for the first time, she meets me halfway, pressing her mouth to mine.

Chapter 16

Lee

The past two weeks, I've kept myself busy by working at the restaurant. It helps the days go by faster.

But the nights remain long.

I light the candle Layla gave me, and like all the nights before, I take three steps back, and then I kneel down. Lowering my head to the floor, I shut my eyes as my heart cries, while I show my mother respect.

Eomma, I miss you.

There's a knock at the door and straightening up, I blow out the candle.

I walk to the door, and when I open it, I see Lake's patient face. I can't help but wonder for how long he'll remain patient with me before he gives up.

Then he smiles at me, and I chastise myself for doubting him when he's never given me any reason to.

I move to the side so he can come in, and I smell his scent as he walks by me.

Slowly, my senses have been returning one by one. The first one was hearing when our group of friends offered me words of encouragement. The second was seeing their comforting smiles. The third was feeling their sincerity.

The fourth… smelling the man who has stood solid as a lighthouse during the storm, never faltering in shining his light so I wouldn't get lost in this long dark night.

When he notices I'm not following him to the couch, Lake comes back, and he closes the door before he takes hold of my shoulders and leans down to catch my eyes. "What are you thinking?"

I take a step forward and lift my hand to his face. Closing my eyes, I let my fingers trail down his temple, over the bristles on his jaw, past his neck, until I flatten my hand over his chest.

His aura is so strong it pierced through the grim shroud of death.

Opening my eyes, I bring them up to his.

"I'm thinking of how lucky I am. You've filled my chest with so many emotions that it overflows, and there's no longer space for my heart." I take a deep breath before I continue, "So I'm giving it to you, Lake. Please... don't ever give it back to me."

Lake closes the distance between us, and he places his hands on my jaw. "I promise," he whispers, and then he presses a soft kiss to my lips.

One day when I'm old, and I've been blessed with grandchildren, I'll tell them the story of how love was born from death.

Lake

Every night for the past two weeks, I would shower and put on a t-shirt and my sweatpants, and then I'd go to Lee and sit with her until she fell asleep.

I expected to do the same thing tonight, to just sit on the couch until she drifted off, and then I'd carry her to bed before I'd leave.

But she just told me she's giving me her heart and it means the world to me. When I pull back after kissing her, the corner of her mouth lifts, and she asks, "Will it be wrong of me to ask you to stay? I just really want to wake up to your face."

Her request makes a smile form around my own mouth. "Of course, I'll stay."

She gets the shy expression on her face, I've missed seeing, and then she darts to her room.

I close my eyes for a second, feeling so damn thankful that my Lee is coming back. Bit by bit, she's returning to her old self as the initial sting of grief lessens.

I switch off the light in the living room, and when I get to the bedroom door, I glance inside, and the sight of Lee staring at the bed with wide eyes while she takes a deep breath makes my smile widen.

I walk inside, asking, "Is there a side you prefer to sleep on?"

"The right side." Her eyes dart from the bed to me, and then she quickly adds, "Unless you like that side."

I let out a chuckle and move toward the left side. "No," and gesturing at the other side, I add, "It's all yours."

When she pauses, I tilt my head to the bed with a patient smile.

Lee lets out a nervous chuckle as she moves forward, and pulling back the covers, she sits down on the side.

I'm going to have to do some serious research on how to get her to relax, and how to lessen the pain of having sex for the first time before we get married.

Which reminds me, we need to talk about the wedding.

I go to turn off the light and walking back to the bed, I toss the covers back and sit down on the mattress. I reach over and grabbing hold of Lee's waist, I pull her toward me. She lets out a cute startled sound when I lie down and wrap my arms around her.

Her wide eyes shine in the nightlight, and her body is tense against mine. Seeing her like this only makes me feel more protective of her.

"Breathe, Lee," I remind her when it sounds like she's holding it.

She lets out a slow breath, but then I reach for the covers, and with a burst of air, Lee whispers, "Eomeo!"

"Let's talk about the wedding," I say. "My mother will be making most of the arrangements. Are you okay with that?"

She nods, and I feel her slightly relaxing against me.

"This coming Wednesday, we'll have dinner with my parents. It's kind of a tradition."

She nods again, and I feel some of her hair tug under my left arm. Moving my arm, I gather all her hair with my other hand, which has her whispering, "I usually braid it, but I forgot tonight."

"Yeah?" I pull my arm free from under her and get up. "Where's your brush?" I ask while I walk to the bathroom and switch on the light.

"It's on the counter by the sink. There's a hair tie wrapped around the handle."

Seeing the brush, I quickly grab it and walking back into the room, Lee sits up.

"Turn the other way," I say as I sit down.

Surprise flashes across her face, but she turns her back to me.

"This is my first time, so I can't promise it's going to look good," I murmur as I pull the brush through her hair before I separate the silky strands into three parts. I weave them together until I get to the end, and after tieing it, I sit back and admire my first attempt. "Not bad, I think it should hold."

She glances at me from over her shoulder, and the sight steals my breath.

Her exotic features are illuminated by the light shining from the bathroom, and it makes her look mysterious and delicate.

She pats her hand over the back of her head, and then she smiles. "Thank you."

I could sit and stare at Lee all night, but she needs her sleep. I get up and place the brush back on the counter, then turn off the light and get back into bed.

This time Lee's more relaxed, and when I open my right arm, she scoots closer and lies down, resting her head on my shoulder.

I wrap my other arm around her lower back and let out a breath before I say, "When I spoke with Je-ha, he said he wants us to get married at an earlier date." I intentionally use his first name, so Lee will know exactly what I think of him.

"He did?" she asks, tilting her head back and looking up at me.

"Are you okay with that?" I ask.

She nods, then whispers, "That would make you my guardian, and he won't have power over my life any longer."

I know it's not her only motivation for agreeing, but I still ask, "Is that the only reason why?"

"No." She snuggles her cheek against my shoulder, then continues, "It would be my honor to become your wife."

As formal as it sounds, I know the meaning behind it, and it fills my heart with peace. Honor and dignity are the most important qualities of Lee's life. For her to say it would be her honor means more to me than hearing her say she loves me.

I press a kiss to her hair. "It's now the end of February. I have to start studying soon if I actually want to graduate. How do you feel about getting married in two weeks?"

She glances up at me again, and a smile curves around her mouth. "I'd like that. Will we stay here after the wedding?"

I nod. "Just until I graduate. After that, we could go to Africa with Falcon and Layla as part of a honeymoon."

"Jinjja?" Her eyes widen with excitement, and it makes me chuckle.

"Yeah, really. I want to talk to Mr. Shepard, Layla's father, because he travels for a living. I think that might be something I'd like to do. Learn about different countries, experience their cultures... I want us to be free."

Lee turns onto her stomach and rests her upper body on her forearms. "What about Falcon and Mason?"

"Mason's starting work soon after graduation and Falcon's already started a business. We can get a house close to them," I grin at the idea. "Like a home base, we can always come back to."

Emotion washes over her face as she admits, "I really like that idea, Lake. You make our future sound wonderful."

Locking eyes with her, I whisper, "I'll always do my best to make you happy, Lee."

The emotion overwhelms her, and it makes her eyes sparkle.

Lee

Has it really been only a couple of weeks?

It feels like Lake has always been a part of me in some way.

"Do you think we met in a past life?" I ask softly.

"If we did, I must've done something right to meet you again in this life." Lake's answer fills me with so much love and appreciation for him.

I lean over him and press a tender kiss to his mouth, then I whisper, "I'll love you so much in this life, the deities will have no choice but to give you back to me in the next life."

Lake moves his hand up to my neck, while his eyes soften with tenderness before he pulls me closer until our mouths touch again.

The first kiss was a learning experience, but this one feels like a promise. His lips part as they caress mine, and when I open mine, his tongue softly brushes against my bottom lip, and it sends a flurry of intense ripples racing over my skin.

Lake pushes me back, so he's half leaning over me, and his tongue brushes alongside my lip again before he slowly enters my mouth. The sensations he creates within me, leaves me marveling at how his touch can feel so different from any other touch. He wakes every cell in my body, and like grass fields sway as they try to keep up with the wind, I lean toward him.

With a wild heartbeat, I imitate the movements of his tongue, and it makes a soft groan escape him.

He brings a hand to my side, and his fingers curl into me. I lift my arms and wrap them around his neck, losing myself in the kiss. Then Lake slips his hand under the hem of my shirt, and feeling his skin against mine has me gasping for my next breath as tingles spread out from the touch.

He pulls me tightly against his body, his hand tracing a tender path up my side, where he stops to tighten his grip over my ribs before he guides his hand to my back, and his fingers trail up my spine.

My body begins to tremble against his as the kiss grows with urgency. Our tongues explore each other, tasting with passionate strokes until we're both breathless and gasping for air.

Lake has to break the kiss and pull back because the intense moment between us has swept me far away to a place where restrictions and rules don't exist.

Chapter 17

Lake

While I'm in class, I hardly hear a word the professor says. My mind keeps drifting to our upcoming wedding and everything we need to do to make sure we succeed in getting rid of Je-ha Park.

I only realize the class is over when the other students get up. I grab my stuff and rush out of the aisle and down the stairs.

I get to the suite before Falcon and Mason, and I quickly shower. Dressing in a suit, I grab a tie and walking out of my room, I call out, "Mason, Falcon, are you ready?"

Falcon comes out of his room while shrugging on his jacket, and seconds later, Mason walks into the living room. He places his watch and cufflinks on the coffee table, then walks over to me. Taking the tie from my hand, he flips my collar up, and while he's busy making the tie, his eyes meet mine. "Today's the day. We're going to get this investment."

Grinning, I say, "You are."

When he's done, he brushes his hands over my shoulders. "No one fucks with my baby brother and gets away with it."

"I'm only five months younger than you," I remind him while a grateful smile lifts the corners of my mouth.

"Let's go. This is one meeting we can't be late for," Falcon says, as he grabs the car keys. "Mason, don't forget your watch and cufflinks. I'll drive so you can put them on."

"The folder," Mason reminds Falcon.

"Fuck, I almost forgot the most important thing." Falcon lets out a chuckle as he jogs back to his room to grab our proposal.

⸻

When we walk into the California branch of Indie Ink Publishing, my stomach begins to churn with nerves.

We take the elevator to the top floor and the doors open to a reception area.

"Good afternoon," the receptionist greets, "How can I help you?"

"Mason Chargill from CRC Holdings to meet with Rhett Daniels," Mason replies.

"Please take a seat while I notify Mr. Daniels."

While we wait, Mason looks over the proposal.

A door at the far end of the hallway opens, and a woman walks out of the office, followed by a man. The woman's clothes are a mismatch of colors, and the heels she's wearing sparkles with every move.

"So it's settled then, my babykins." She excitedly claps her hands. "Ohhh, I can't wait. I'll finally have all my chunks of hunks in one place at the same time. I've worked the sparkle clear out of my bedazzled ass to make this happen, so you better not call me with an excuse."

I begin to chuckle and try to cover it up with a cough, but then Falcon snorts next to me, and all hope is lost as I crack up.

Mason tries to compose his face and remain businesslike, but when I start wheezing, he covers his face and begins to laugh as well, while groaning, "We're so fucked."

"Worked the... sparkle... clear out... of my... my... my..." I can't finish the sentence as I gasp for air.

"Bedazzled ass," the woman says right by me.

I try to give her an apologetic look but epically fail. She watches me with a huge smile, and tilting her head, she says, "My babykins, I approve of whatever business you want to do with this fine-looking chunk of hunk."

"Oh... my... god..." I gasp as tears begin to roll down my face. "Can't... breathe."

"We're so sorry," Mason gets out between bouts of laughter.

"Aw fuck, Rhett. How could you let Miss Sebastian get to them first," another guy says as he walks toward us.

"I dare you to try and stop her, Jax," Rhett says, and crossing his arms, he watches us with a wide grin.

Mason manages to recover first, and rising to his feet, he introduces himself," Mason Chargill and I apologize for the unprofessional behavior." Glancing back at me and Falcon, he adds, "Lake Cutler and Falcon Reyes."

Falcon clears his throat then goes to shake their hands while I pray I can keep the laughter in just so I can greet them.

"Rhett Daniels. Thank you for reaching out to us. Our CEO, Carter Hayes, and another director, Logan West, couldn't be here today." Rhett turns to the other man, "This is Jaxson West." Then he glances over his shoulder, "and the late one is Marcus Reed."

"Rhett Daniels, I will knock the grumpy right out of you. How's Marcus late? We're all still standing here," Miss Sebastian scolds.

I lift my hand in a hopeless gesture as I sink down to my knees.

"It's okay," Jaxson says. "We've been there."

"What do you mean by that, Jaxson West." Miss Sebastion places one hand on her hip while the other hand darts up, and sticking her pointer finger in the air, she wags it right in front of Jaxson's face. "I will kick your fine ass to the high heavens. Don't you go using that sassing tone when you're talking about my bedazzled ass."

Today is the day I laugh myself into an early grave.

Once I manage to breathe again, Miss Sebastian says, "Before you start your meeting, I'd like to invite y'all over to my place for a little B & D on Saturday." She glares at Jaxson as he begins to lean toward Rhett. "And no, it does not stand for boobs and dicks. Does your mind have a permanent zip code in the gutter?"

"Shit, you're going to kill me," I wheeze.

"Oh, honey, I can do this all day long just to hear you laugh." She leans closer to me and whispers, "But my chunks of hunks will tan my hide bright red and being a married woman and all, I can't go doing kinky things behind my hubby's back."

"If you don't stop her, we're going to have to call 911 because he's about to pass out from lack of air," Marcus says to Rhett.

"Get your fine ass out of here, woman. You're going to kill our prospective partners," Rhett growls, and it doesn't help at all.

I grab at my chest, pretty sure I'm going to have a heart attack soon.

"Aaannnyyywwwaaayyy." She rolls her eyes at Rhett before she looks at us. "The impatient chunk of hunk will give you my address. See ya all on Saturday."

Her eyes zero in on Mason, and she first looks him over, which has his laughter drying up faster than the speed of light. "Bring an oxygen tank for my chucklelicious on the floor. He's going to need it."

***

Lee

While Lake's at a meeting, I begin to get ready for dinner with his parents. I want to complement Lake tonight and show his parents their son has made the right choice – and that they have made the right choice by arranging our marriage.

I take my time, washing my hair, and going through my skincare routine, which I've gotten used to over the past couple of weeks. Before coming here, I'd just wash my face, put on sunscreen, and then dart out the door. But Preston went through a lot of effort to get the products for me, so I'll use every last drop.

I'm busy drying my hair when there's a knock at the door. When I open it, Layla and Kingsley walk inside. I shut the door and watch as Kingsley lays a peach-colored dress over the couch. Layla disappears into my bedroom with a bag over her shoulder, calling out, "The men have their meeting, and we have ours. Let's get started."

"Started?" I ask Kingsley as we follow Layla into the bedroom.

"We're going to make you look so hot, Lake's going to dissolve into a puddle of drool," Kingsley teases.

"Eomeo!" I press my hands to my cheeks. "I want to impress his parents, not make them second guess their decision to let me marry their son."

Layla lets out a chuckle, then she looks at me. "Oh good, you've washed your hair already. We came just in time. I love how in sync we all are."

Kingsley brings the chair from the desk in the living room and places it in the bathroom. Then she pushes me toward it, and once I sit down, they both get to work. Layla dries my hair, and Kingsley starts with my makeup.

A couple of minutes later, Layla lets our a burst of laughter. "You should see your faces. Whenever

Kingsley pouts, you pout. If she raises her eyebrows, you do the same. It's so cute."

My eyes dart from Kingsley to Layla's reflection in the mirror, feeling so thankful for them.

Lake's family and friends are becoming my family and friends. It makes me feel like the richest person on earth.

Lake

"That was the best meeting I've ever been to," I mumble from the back seat.

"You can say that again," Falcon agrees.

"Guys," Mason says, "Do you realize what just happened?"

"You got the investment," I say, my voice filled with relief. "You did it."

"We did it," Mason corrects me.

"We fucking did it," Falcon adds.

Mason slaps a hand against the steering wheel while he shouts, "Hell yeah!"

I lean back against the seat and cover my face with my hands as emotion washes over me, flooding my eyes with tears. I feel utter relief that I can tell Park to fuck off, and overwhelming gratefulness for Mason and Falcon, because without them I'd be half the man I am today. And love… so much love for Lee.

"Buddy, are you crying?" Mason asks.

"Do you blame me?"

"Not one bit. I feel like crying myself," he admits.

When we drive through the gates of Trinity Academy, I think of the profound way our lives have changed this past year. Our group grew. Lee, Layla, Kingsley, and Preston taught us so much.

Mason dealt with Jen's death.

Falcon reunited with Julian and Mr. Reyes.

And me… I finally realized what I wanted to do with my future.

I glance over my shoulder to where West's car went over, and I feel a pang of guilt for not remembering him sooner. Our lives went on while his ended.

Wherever you are, I hope Jennifer found you. I hope she gave you the forgiveness and peace you were looking for.

Looking back in front of me, my eyes go to The Hope Diamond, and I smile.

Grandpa, I now understand why you called it The Hope Diamond. I've found mine, and she's up there waiting for me right now.

Chapter 18

Lake

I knock on Lee's door, and when Layla opens the door, I grin. "I'm here for my fiancée."

"Brace yourself, Lake," she says, a proud look on her face. "She's going to sweep your feet from under you."

"Yeah, what did you do?" I ask as I step inside.

I shut the door behind me, and as I turn to look at Layla, movement from the bedroom door catches my eye.

And then I forget to breathe.

I can only stare for a moment.

Lee's wearing a light, peach-colored dress with three-quarter sleeves and a square neckline. Silk pads the lace down to her thighs, and then it's just a waterfall of lace.

I have to pull my collar away from my neck as I take in her legs.

"What do you think?" Layla asks.

"I'm still looking," I mumble as my eyes drift back up to her face. The girls curled her hair at the ends, and my eyes get stuck on one curl as it follows the curve of her breast.

"Don't move," I say quickly while I yank out my phone. I take a photo of her because I'm *really* not done looking.

"Aww crap, I got candy stuck in my tooth," Kingsley complains.

"And there's one of the reasons I almost remained a single father," I mumble as I walk toward Lee.

Layla cracks up behind me, and I smirk because I can't wait to see what affect Miss Sebastian is going to have on the girls.

Stopping in front of Lee, I reach for her hand. I have to force my eyes to stay on her face because, with my height, I have a perfect view of her cleavage.

"You look breathtaking," I whisper, and then I lean down and press a kiss to the corner of her mouth, so I don't ruin her makeup.

Lee tugs at the bodice of the dress, giving me a worried glance. "The dress is so low. Won't it offend your parents?"

"No," the word bursts from me. "Definitely not. You look perfect in the dress."

Everything looks perfect in the dress.

"We're going to leave you two love birds," Kingsley says as she squeezes past us. "Enjoy dinner with the folks."

"Thank you for helping me get ready," Lee calls out after them.

When the door shuts behind them, I take two steps back and let my gaze slowly drift over her again.

"I think you should just permanently keep the dress on from now on," I tease.

"We should go," Lee says with a smile.

When she walks by me, and I see her from behind, I let out a groan. "Freeze quickly." Pulling out my phone again. "I have to take another photo because that ass needs to be framed."

Lee

Layla, Kingsley, and I are all sitting in the guys' suite waiting for them to finish getting ready so we can go to the BBQ that's being held by their new partners.

After having dinner with Lake's parents, I felt much better. They were just as warm and kind as Lake.

Mrs. Cutler kept assuring me everything concerning the wedding is taken care of. She got a wedding planner to handle the event.

I'm grateful but sad at the same time. I would've preferred a more intimate and traditional ceremony to celebrate the union of my and Lake's love.

I keep glancing around the suite because it's the first time I've been in it.

"Are you looking for something?" Kingsley asks.

I quickly shake my head. "It's my first time in this suite."

"What?" Layla gives me a shocked look. "Lake hasn't brought you up here yet?"

I shake my head again, smiling at her.

"Lake!" Kingsley yells at the top of her lungs.

"What?" Lake comes out of the room, strapping a watch to his wrist.

"Why haven't you brought Lee up here yet?" she asks.

"I have," he frowns then looks at me, "haven't I?"

"No." I let out a chuckle when shock settles over his face.

"Oh wait," he says. "It's because I share it with Falcon and Mason, and we would have zero privacy."

"Oooh... why do you need privacy?" Kingsley teases him.

"To plan how I'm going to ship y'all off to boarding school," Lake jokes as he walks toward me. He holds his hand out to me, and when I take it, he pulls me to my feet so fast, I crash into his chest. Grinning down at me, he teases, "Let me show you my bedroom."

"Kids don't wanna hear no noises," Kingsley shouts after us as Lake pulls me into his room.

He shuts the door and taking hold of my hips, he pushes me back against the wood, and then he whispers, "Finally."

"Finally?" I ask.

He tilts his head to the right, and his mouth pulls into a smirk that does things to my insides and holds my eyes hostage.

"I finally have you alone for a second," he whispers, and then his mouth presses against mine.

My eyes instantly drift shut because the kiss is so intense, I can't focus on anything else but it.

Lake thrusts his tongue into my mouth, and then he brushes hard strokes over mine until it feels like my legs are going to give way beneath me, and I have to grab hold of his shoulders to remain standing. His body pushes harder against mine as his hands move up my sides.

"Let's go!" Mason yells.

I was so caught up in the kiss the sudden shout has me jerking with fright. Lake pulls away and rests his forehead against the door while I stare at his chest as I try to catch my breath.

"We are definitely staying in your suite after the wedding," he grumbles, and it makes laughter bubble over my lips.

When we're both breathing normally again, Lake links his fingers with mine, and we leave his room.

"We can't take the Bently," Falcon says.

Mason frowns. "Why?"

"How are we all going to fit?"

"Lee can sit on my lap," Lake says as he pulls me back against his chest and wraps his arms around the front of me, resting his chin on top of my head.

"You guys look so cute right now," Kingsley says, a wide grin on her face.

"We're taking the Bently." Falcon grabs the keys, then adds, "Mason can drive, then Layla can sit on my lap."

"There's no fucking way I'm driving your asses all over town while you're making out in the back seat."

Lake holds his hand out to Falcon. "Daddy will drive while the kids make out."

"Aww…" Kingsley blows him a kiss. "We have the best parents."

When everyone is finally in the car, and Lake steers it through the gates of the Academy, Mason grumbles, "Hunt, your bony ass is stabbing into my leg."

"You love my bony ass," she sasses him back.

We listen to them bicker until Lake parks the car in front of a beautiful house. There are so many colorful flowers in the garden; it makes everything look cheerful.

I get out of the car and chuckle when Falcon and Layla almost fall out.

"Ooooo. Mmmmm. Ggggg!"

My head snaps toward the screeching woman, and then my eyes widen as she comes storming across the road. She's heading right for me, and I press myself back against the car.

"You're a real-life angel-doll!" she shrieks with so much excitement, and then she grabs hold of me and yanks me to her.

I suck in a breath of air but instantly begin to cough when I only get a lung full of perfume.

My eyes dart to Layla for help, but she's staring at the woman with wide eyes and parted lips. Falcon begins to chuckle, and then I hear Lake and Mason laugh.

Luckily Lake comes to my rescue, and he pulls me to him, freeing me from the woman.

"She's yours?" the woman asks, and I nod before Lake can even answer, which has Mason laughing harder.

"Hi, Miss Sebastian," Lake greets her.

Miss Sebastian leans right over me and hugs Lake, and it has me holding my breath until she pulls back.

"An angel-doll for my chucklelicious. Bestill my swooning heart," Miss Sebastian coos.

I get a moment to look at her face, and then a smile splits over mine. "You're Asian?"

"Momma's side comes from Taiwan. Unfortunately, Momma didn't have good taste, and she hooked up with a good-for-nothing pavement special." She inclines her head, then says, "Wang Kao, aka Sebastian Ward, but you can just call me Miss Sebastian."

I bow my head. "Park Lee-ann. Just call me Lee."

"Woman!" A man shouts from the other side of the road. "Can you at least let them come in before you bombard them?"

"Rhett Daniels!" she shrieks as she spins around and stalks toward him. "Don't you dare raise your voice at me. I will kick you right in the sparklies and make you sound like you have a helium balloon stuck up your ass."

Lake begins to laugh, and feeling his body shake against mine makes my smile widen.

"Ooh kinky," Rhett says to her. "Is that a promise?"

She shoves at him, but he only staggers back two steps before he grabs hold of her and yanks her against him.

"Oh, holy mother of fashion. My heels! You're making me scrape my heels against the paving!"

Lake laughs so hard, he drops his forehead to my shoulder, and he has to lean back against the car to stay upright.

Kingsley keeps snorting, and it makes laughter burst over my lips.

Chapter 19

Lake

We've been at the BBQ for ten minutes, and my stomach already aches from all the laughter.

Suddenly a little girl comes running out of the house, shrieking, "Uncle Ledge!"

Rhett throws the tongs at Jaxson, who manages to catch it. Turning to the girl, Rhett holds his arms open, and the girl jumps, flinging herself at him. "Fuck, Princess. I missed you."

A girl who could easily be the same age as Lee comes out, shouting, "I heard that. A hundred dollars in the swear jar."

"Jamie, are you still saving for college?" Marcus asks her.

She wags her brows at him. "I'm hoping Carter will pay, and I can use it for something else. The way you all keep cursing up a storm, I'll be able to buy my first house with cash."

More people arrive, and Marcus begins to introduce us. When everyone has arrived, I'm so confused, I lean over to Miss Sebastian, and ask, "Who's who again?"

She clears her throat and points at Carter. "Carter, Jaxson, Marcus, Logan and my babykins, Rhett, are all best friends. Della's married to Carter and Danny's their daughter. Jamie is Della's sister." She pauses and gives me a stern look. "Are you still with me on the crazy train?"

"Yes," I chuckle.

"Evie is married to Rhett. Willow is married to Marcus. Leigh is married to Jaxson, and she's my bestie. Mia is married to Logan, and she's also Rhett's sister."

Miss Sebastian scowls as her eyes sweep over everyone. "I think I covered it all. It confused me like a hamster in a bigass dryer in the beginning. That's why I call them my chunk of hunks and my angel-girls. It was easier just doing that until I figured out who was who and which magic wand went into which cave of wonder."

I crack up, and it has Miss Sebastian patting my back as I hunch over while she sips on her cosmopolitan.

"He needs air, Miss Sebastian," Marcus scolds her.

"You better watch yourself, Marcus Reed. Just because I washed your ding dong a couple of times, it doesn't mean you can take that tone with me."

Marcus starts nodding and holds up his beer. "Thanks for that. Now everyone knows."

"What's wrong with that?" She stands up and wiggles her finger in front of him. "Are you ashamed of the special moments we shared?"

"I didn't say that at all." Marcus places his arm around her shoulder, then looks at me. "She held my heart in her hands."

I blink a couple of times before I ask, "Figuratively?"

He shakes his head. "No, she's one of two people who literally held my heart in their hands."

"Long story short," Miss Sebastian jumps in. "His bedazzled ass was on the bullet train to Valhalla when Leigh, my bestie, performed a miracle, and I assisted her during the operation."

"Are you serious?" I ask, surprised by the story.

Marcus nods. "Yeah, that about sums it up."

"Wow," I breathe. "And you're better now?"

"Oh yeah." Marcus gestures to Leigh. "Besides, if anything goes wrong down the road, I have the best cardiothoracic surgeon in the world."

"She's that good?" I ask as my eyes go to Leigh.

"She's a genius."

"Oh, we have one of those too," Kingsley pops in. I wasn't even aware she was listening.

"Yeah, Preston. His specialty lies more in computers," I say, and then I wonder why I haven't seen him around.

"Where is Preston?" I ask no one in particular.

"He's writing exams," Falcon answers.

"Already?" I ask.

"Didn't I tell you? Preston's doing his four-year degree in two years so he can finish earlier. I need him full time for the new business."

"You started a new business?" Carter suddenly asks.

Knowing where this conversation is heading, I stand up and offer Carter my chair. "Take the seat."

I walk over to where Lee is talking to Layla, then Kingsley bumps me as she darts by me and teasingly say, "Thanks for leaving me at the business meeting."

Wrapping my arms around Lee from behind, I look at my group before I glance at our new friends, and it feels like I'm getting a preview of our future.

***

Lee

It's the night before our wedding, and even though I'm happy to marry Lake tomorrow, I can't help but feel down.

My mom won't be there, and it won't be traditional.

It just doesn't feel right.

My phone beeps, and when I unlock the screen, I see a message from Layla.

Can you please come help me with something in my suite?"

Glad for the distraction, I practically dart out of my suite, and within seconds I'm knocking on her door.

Layla opens the door and grabbing my hand, she yanks me inside.

"What's wrong?" I ask.

Layla takes hold of my shoulders, and she pushes me toward her bedroom. When I walk through the door, both my hands fly up to cover my mouth and tears push up my throat.

"You got me a hanbok," I whisper in awe. Walking closer, I brush my fingers lightly over the silk. "Where did you get it?"

Layla places her arm around my waist and hugs me. "I went looking for it when we were in Jeju. I wanted you to have a traditional wedding gown."

"Layla, it's so beautiful." I turn to her and hug her with all of my strength. "Thank you so much."

I pull back and kneeling down at the foot of the bed, I brush my hand over the dress. The light pink material shimmers in the electric light.

"You better get dressed," Layla says.

"Now?" I ask, climbing to my feet again.

"Yes." Layla takes a deep breath, and her eyes begin to shine. "We're having a private ceremony tonight. Just our group."

In a daze of wonderment and pure bliss, Layla helps me get ready. Every couple of seconds, I have to cover my mouth and take deep breaths, so I don't start crying.

After I've pinned my hair up, and Layla's changed into a flowing lilac-colored dress, she holds her arm out for me. I swallow hard as I take hold of her, and we leave her suite.

When we walk out of the building, my breath catches in my throat. There are little lanterns all along the path, and as we follow them, Layla says, "Thank you for loving Lake."

I nod because I'm too emotional to say anything.

The lanterns lead us into the woods, through the tunnel of trees, and when we reach the open space that looks out over the valley, I see Falcon, Mason, and Preston standing by Lake's side. He looks devastatingly handsome in his dark suit.

When my eyes move to the left, and I see Kingsley, I can't hold back the tears. I glance away and take deep breaths before I walk closer to her. I incline my head to her, and then my eyes go to the beautifully framed photo of my mom that they've put on a stand.

I kneel down in front of my mother, and I bow to the ground, showing her that I will always respect her.

"Eomeoni, salanghaeyo," I whisper before I climb back to my feet with Kingsley and Layla's help.

I keep my eyes lowered as I walk to Lake, and when I stop a few steps in front of him, my heart takes flight like a lantern set free with all my wishes written on it.

I bow low to Lake, showing him how committed I am to him, and I have to take deep breaths when Lake bows to me.

We straighten up, and he gives me the gentlest of smiles. "Park Lee-ann, my life changed the day you walked into it. You're the greatest source of inspiration I have ever known. You inspire me to follow my dreams. You inspire me to fight for those I love. Mostly, you inspire me to be a better man. I will do my best as your husband." He takes a deep breath, then he repeats my words from the other night, "I'll love you so much in this life, the deities will have no choice but to give you back to me in the next life."

There's a moment's silence before I say, "Lake Cutler, you are the most unexpected and greatest gift of my life." I take a couple of breaths so I won't start crying. "During the dark night of my soul, you were my lighthouse. Your light shone through the storm so I wouldn't lose my way. With a gentle heart, you've taught me that any bridge can be crossed. You have filled my soul with riches, and for that, I vow my life to you. I will love you so much in this life, the deities will have no choice but to give you back to me in the next life, and the life thereafter, because no life is worth living if you are not by my side."

When we have finished our vows, Layla brings a gourd, and each of the sides has wine in them.

With two hands, I receive one from her, and when Lake has his, we drink the wine together, showing that we are now two halves coming together as one.

When the ceremony is completed, I smile up at Lake, and my heart is at peace, knowing my mom must be proud of me for marrying such an honorable man.

"Fuck. Lake just got married," Mason suddenly whispers, his face filling with shock.

"Are you being serious right now?" Kingsley asks. "You were standing right there while they were saying their vows."

"I know, but it just suddenly hit me," Mason explains.

Falcon pats him on the shoulder. "Don't worry, I felt it too."

Lake places his arm around my waist and leaning down, he whispers, "You're the most beautiful bride in the world. Thank you for becoming my wife."

Standing on my toes, I wrap my arms around his neck. "Salanghaeyo, Lake."

Chapter 20

Lake

Last night I wore a royal blue suit with a purple tie. The blue represented my mother, whereas the purple represented Lee's mother. Today I'm wearing a black suit my mother had tailor-made for me.

Standing by the door, I welcome the guests, and when the guest of honor arrives, I incline my head to him and his mistress. "Chairman Park, thank you for gracing us with your presence today."

"Mr. Cutler," he says, his mouth set in a victorious smile.

I watch them walk to my father, Mr. Chargill, and Mr. Reyes.

Dad glances at me, and I nod, indicating that we're ready.

Mason comes to stand slightly behind me, and whispers, "It's showtime."

"Let's do this." I walk to the front where Falcon is standing by the table that's been set up for us to sign the marriage license.

My father approaches the table with Mr. Park and gestures for him to take a seat, and Mr. Reyes takes the other.

I watch as Mr. Park reads the document, and glancing up, I see Mason and Kingsley waiting next to the aisle. My eye catches Kingsley's, and when she smiles at me, I feel a little of the tension ebb away.

Layla and my mother are with Lee, so I know she's in good hands, and I can give my full attention to this moment.

Mr. Park finally reaches the last page, and he proudly signs his name on the dotted line. Mr. Reyes signs beneath him, and Mr. Chargill and dad sign as witnesses.

When the men shake hands, Falcon steps closer, pretending to assist his father to his feet so he can be right by the table and ready to switch the blank contract with the signed one, the instant Kingsley distracts Je-ha.

Then after Je-ha has signed the marriage license, I can tell him to go to hell, and the signed contract will be destroyed.

Mr. Park gets up and adjusts his jacket with a smug look. He walks around the table toward the aisle, and I subtly walk to the front of the table, blocking the mistress' view, just in case she glances this way.

Kingsley begins to walk and glancing over her shoulder, she says, "You know I love you more than chocolate." And then she slams into Mr. Park, and I actually cringe when they both fall into a line of chairs. Luckily, Kingsley landed on top of Mr. Park, and she pushes him down when he tries to get up. "Oops," she exclaims. She pretends to lose her balance and almost elbows him in the groin. "So sorry."

"I don't think that was an accident," Falcon says. "It's a pity she missed."

Falcon gives Mason the sign, and he rushes forward to help Kingsley up. "Babe, are you okay?" he pretends to fuss over her, and wrapping his arms around her, he hugs her tight before they walk to the front row.

"Mission accomplished," Falcon whispers. "I've swapped the contract for the fake one."

"Now for the grand finale," I say as I walk to the front and take my place.

Dad comes to stand next to me. "That went better than I thought it would."

"Thanks to everyone," I say as I give Kingsley a thankful smile.

Making a heart shape with her fingers, she winks at me.

When all the guests are seated, a pianist plays the opening notes to *Kiss the rain* composed by *Yurima*. My mother went through so much trouble to make today special for Lee and me.

Layla opens the doors and then comes to sit up front next to Falcon.

When my mother appears with Lee on her arm, emotions swamp me from all sides. They walk toward us as the light piano notes fill the air, and once again, Lee is the most beautiful bride.

She's wearing a white lace dress my mother had made for her, and it makes her look like an angel as she glides toward me.

"How lucky am I that I get to marry her twice?" I whisper to my father.

"You deserve this and so much more, my son. It's been an absolute honor to watch you grow into a man."

I glance up at the ceiling and take deep breaths, so I won't start crying like a baby in front of Lee.

When my mom and Lee reach us, the minister asks, "Who gives this woman away?"

Mom smiles as she takes hold of Lee's hand in a tight grip. "On behalf of her mother, Park Soo-jin, I do."

"Thank you," I whisper to Mom. If she didn't ask Park Je-ha for this favor, then he would be the one saying, I do.

Mom takes a step back, and Lee and I turn to face the minister. I take hold of her hand and pull it through the crook of my arm.

The minister reads a short passage, and then we turn to face each other.

Dad gives me Lee's ring while Mom gives Lee the ring that's meant for me. I had the set made so we would have unique rings to represent our once in a lifetime love for each other.

I clear my throat, and as I hold the ring in front of Lee's third finger, I say, "With this ring, I Lake Cutler, take you, Park Lee-ann, to be my lawfully wedded wife, to have and to hold, from this day forward, for better, for worse, for richer, for poorer, in sickness and in health, until death do us part.

A happy smile shines on Lee's face when I push the ring onto her finger.

She takes hold of my left hand, and says, "I, Park Lee-ann, take you, Lake Cutler, to be my lawfully wedded husband, to have and to hold, from this day forward, for better, for worse, for richer, for poorer, in sickness and in health, until death do us part.

She takes a deep breath, and a chuckle escapes from me while she pushes the ring onto my finger.

Soon after, the minister announces, "Therefore, in accordance with the law of Califonia, it is truly my pleasure to pronounce you husband and wife. Lake, you may kiss your beautiful wife."

I turn to Lee, and for a moment, I just look at the woman who has become my every heartbeat. I bring a hand to her jaw and brush my thumb over her cheek. "I love you, Lee-ann Cutler."

Tears fill her eyes, and each one sparkles with happiness. I press a soft kiss to her mouth, and as I pull back, she whispers, "I love you, my husband."

Taking her hand, I link our fingers, and we walk over to the table, I help her sit down, and I take the seat next to her. When Mr. Park joins us, the minister shows Lee where to sign, and I sign my signature next to hers.

Dad signs as my witness, and then I hold my breath until Mr. Park has signed as Lee's witness.

When his signature is complete, a dizzying wave of relief flows through me, and I squeeze Lee's hand beneath the table.

The minister takes the marriage license, and I wait until everyone has left the hall, except for our small group, before I rise to my feet.

Lee

Lake helps me up from the chair and immediately places an arm around me as we turn to face Park Je-ha.

Mr. Reyes walks toward us with his eldest son, and says, "Je-ha, I forgot to tell you the good news." He turns and places an arm around his son's shoulders. "I retired at the end of last year. My eldest was inaugurated in November."

My eyes dart to Park Je-ha, and I watch as he glances down at the papers on the table.

Lake picks up the papers and smiling he holds it out to Park Je-ha, and says, "CRC Holdings will not be doing any business with you. Your business has been blacklisted with all of our partners. Take your money and shove it up your ass."

He slams the papers against Park Je-ha's chest. "You should've listened to me when I told you, I might be the quiet one, but that doesn't make me the weakest."

Park Je-ha looks through the document, and only the top couple of pages have words printed on them, after that, the pages are all blank.

"Where's the contract I signed?" he asks with restrained anger lacing his words.

Lake gestures with his hand to the right of us. "It's showtime, Mace."

Glancing over my shoulder, I watch as Mason shreds a document with a huge smile on his face.

"You married my daughter and then withdraw from our deal," Park Je-ha grinds the words out. "Do you think I will not retaliate?"

"Oh shit, my bad," Lake chuckles. "I wasn't aware you had a daughter." Lake pulls away from me and steps closer to Je-ha. "Fathers don't leave their daughters to raise themselves. Fathers don't trade their daughters like cattle." He takes another step closer, and I notice how his hands fist at his sides. "You killed her mother in front of her. You are not her fucking father. You're nothing but a piece of shit who thinks his wealth gives him the power to abuse and to kill. I dare you to retaliate. I have three of the most powerful families in the United States standing behind me. Tell me, Je-ha... who do you have?"

Je-ha's eyes dart to his mistress, and it makes Lake glance over his shoulder at her.

"Oh, right. It must be true what they say – shit attracts shit. I hope she was worth the fuck because she just cost you billions."

Jo Yoon-ha must understand English because she gets up and rushes toward me from the aisles of chairs, "Ya! Michin Nyeon!"

I'm so glad I'm wearing flat shoes, and the dress isn't heavy. I grab hold of the lace and stepping around the table, I see the surprise on her face when I dart toward her.

The running start gives me the momentum I need, and then I gather all the anger and shame she has inflicted on me, and I force it to flow through my body as I jump. The kick I deliver to her chest lifts her off the ground for a moment before she crashes back into the chairs.

I was so focused on kicking her, I forgot about the rest of the move, and I fall with a hard thud. Lying on the floor, I stare up at the ceiling with a huge smile on my face.

Then Lake's face appears in my line of sight, and grinning, he says, "That was badass."

"I got carried away, but it was totally worth the fall," I say as he helps me up.

Je-ha stalks toward us, and it has me stepping in front of Lake.

"You have brought shame to the family name!" he shouts at me in Hangul.

"I have done no such thing," I answer him in English, refusing to give him the respect of speaking to him with honorifics. "Your name never meant anything to me." I step closer to him, "I renounce you, Park Je-ha." I smile at him, this man who almost destroyed me, and it brings me great satisfaction as I say, "I renounce your name and family heritage."

Rage burns from his eyes, but I don't lower mine, not today, not ever again.

When he begins to raise his arm, I don't think, but react. I remember my mother's last moments as I grab hold of his arm with my left hand while slamming the palm of my right hand up into his chin. I immediately let go of him and take a step back as he slumps to the ground.

"Now that's what I call a knockout," Mr. Reyes says from behind me. As he walks by us, mumbles, "Good. Good."

Mr. Cutler places his hand on Lake's shoulder and whispers, "Remember what she just did to him when you decide to pick a fight."

Lake reaches for my hand and pulls me to his side. "Should we go celebrate?" he asks as we step around Je-ha.

Chapter 21

Lake

Sitting at the reception at the country club after all the speeches have been made and people begin to eat, I pull Lee's chair closer to mine.

Leaning in, I whisper, "Can I tell you a secret?"

She nods, and lifting her face, she whispers, "What?"

"I've never been this happy before."

She smiles and presses a kiss to my cheek. "Me too."

My eyes scan over the crowd, and then they stop on Clare. "I'll be right back," I say to Lee. "I just need to talk to someone quickly."

"Okay."

Getting up, I glance to where Falcon and Mason are sitting and making sure they're not looking my way, I quickly walk to where Clare is talking to one of the other socialites.

Taking hold of her elbow, I smile when she looks at me. "Oh, Lake. I was giving you a moment with your bride before I came to congratulate you."

"Thank you for being so considerate. Can we talk for a moment?" I ask, keeping my smile polite.

"Of course."

I steer her around the corner and down the stairs. Tucking my left hand in my pocket, I pull out my phone and open the voice recording app. I press record before I slip it back inside my pocket.

"Let's sit over there on the bench," I say.

I sit down on the right side, so the phone is closer to her. As soon as she makes herself comfortable, she turns her curious gaze on me.

"What would you like to talk about?"

"I'm worried, Mrs. Reyes. I'm sure it's nothing, but I thought I should ask for advice, seeing as I've never had to deal with a situation like this before."

My words totally ensnare her, and she leans closer. "Oh no, how awful. I'll help in any way I can."

Forgive me, Layla. I need to tell a white lie.

"I've seen less and less of Falcon, and it really worries me. It's as if… how can I say this." I pretend to hesitate and giving Clare a pleading face, I continue, "Since he got involved with Layla, he's slowly changing, as if she's…"

"Brainwashing him," Clare completes my sentence.

I nod and let out a heavy sigh.

This is for Falcon and Layla. Cry if you have to. Just get her to talk.

"I'm so worried. He's like a brother to me. I can't just do nothing."

"She takes after her mother," Clare sneers. "Stephanie has been trying for years to steal Warren from me." The glass of wine in her hand is forgotten as she continues, "I can't say I blame Miss Shepard. Falcon is a sought after bachelor. He is handsome, wealthy, and comes from one of the most powerful bloodlines. Any woman would want him. My poor child."

Right.

I lean forward and cover my eyes with my hand. "I just wish there was a way to get Falcon away from her or to get rid of her." I take a couple of quick breaths, then whisper, "It's killing me. I'd do anything to get Falcon back."

Clare places her hand on my back and pats me like I'm a damn dog.

"There might be a way. The first time was a huge failure, though."

I rub my eyes before I sit back, and I give Clare the saddest look I can conjure up at the moment. "Tell me. Please, Mrs. Reyes. I'll do anything for Falcon."

"Miss Shepard has a minor allergy, as you know, after the fiasco at the Thanksgiving event. I should've made sure Serena gave her the damn pie when Stephanie wasn't around. That damn EpiPen ruined days worth of planning."

"So, you're saying I should…"

Say it. Please. Say it.

"Just get her to eat something with strawberries. Apparently, you only need a tiny amount for it to do the trick, and then she'll be out of his life for good." She lets out an irritated sigh, then sneers, "After all, it's not murder if you're taking out the trash."

I close my eyes for a moment, so I don't commit *murder* on my wedding day.

She misreads my reaction to her words and pats my back again. "If anyone can help Falcon, it's you, Lake. You're like a son to me. I trust you'll do what's best for Falcon."

Needing just a little bit more information so things can't be taken out of context in a court, I ask, "Where did Serena get the pie, Mrs. Reyes? Layla ate quite a bit of it. She didn't realize it had strawberries in it."

Clare lets out a burst of laughter. "I got it from the bakery. You should try their eclairs. Positively to die for."

"So, I should just do the same thing you told Serena to do?"

"Yes, get the pie, or anything with strawberries. Get Miss Shepard to eat it. Preferably when she's alone, so no one can rush her to the hospital again. We want it to work this time." Clare lets out a sigh. "If only I could get rid of Stephanie that easily. One of these days, I might just lose my patience and run her over with the Rolls Royce." She lets out a chuckle. "Accidents happen so easily these days."

Yeah, they do.

"Thank you for all the advice. You're a lifesaver," I say while getting up. "I better get back before someone realizes I'm gone."

"You're welcome, dear. I'm always willing to lend an ear."

"Enjoy the rest of the reception," I say as I begin to walk away. When I reach the stairs, I keep walking straight ahead until I find a quiet spot. I first make sure there's no one around, and then I pull my phone out and stop the recording.

Please.

I press play and then listen to the confession I just managed to get out of Clare, and I begin to chuckle.

"Oh, Clare, you're so fucked."

I hurry back to the reception and walk straight to Falcon and Mason. "Guys, can I have a minute?"

"Sure," Falcon says, rising from his seat. Mason gets up, and we walk in the direction of the golf course.

"I don't think we can play golf right now," Mason says.

When we're far enough from the guests, I first glance around us before I take my phone out.

"I'm sending you a voice clip just in case something happens to my phone."

"A voice clip?" Falcon asks.

"It's my way of saying thank you for always protecting me," I say to Falcon, and then I look at Mason, "and for always having my back."

Mason gives me a questioning look, and when the message pops up on his phone, he presses play.

I lean closer and fast forward toward the end. "This is the part that matters most."

'Yes, get the pie, or anything with strawberries. Get Miss Shepard to eat it. Preferably when she's alone, so no one can rush her to the hospital again. We want it to work this time. If only I could get rid of Stephanie that easily. One of these days, I might just lose my patience and run her over with the Rolls Royce. Accidents happen so easily these days.'

"Holy fuck, Lake," Mason breathes.

"That's a confession, right?" Falcon asks.

"Not only do we have a confession, but we also have her plotting murder," I say. "That's some serious jail time right there."

I watch as the realization hits Falcon, and he whispers, "She's going to pay."

I lock eyes with Mason. "It also means Serena doesn't have a get-out-of-jail-for-free-card anymore."

Mason shakes his head, then closes his eyes. "Do you have any idea what you've done?" He darts forward and grabs me around the neck in a tight hug. "Thank you." I hug him back, just feeling grateful I could help in some way. "You helped me keep my promise to Kingsley. Thank you."

Falcon hugs me from behind, and then I mumble, "If someone sees us, they're totally going to get the wrong idea."

"Oh yeah?" Mason chuckles. "Should I throw in a hip thrust for added effect?"

"Don't you fucking dare," I grumble, shoving him off of me.

"I can just see the headline in the newspaper tomorrow; how close is too close? CRC threesome on the golf course."

Falcon cracks up, and with his arm around my shoulders, we begin to walk back.

"Fuck, we make a great team," Mason murmurs.

"I have a new pact for us," I say.

"Yeah? Let's hear it," Falcon replies.

"If we ever split up, I'll kick your damn assess," Mason suddenly grumbles.

"That caught the gist of what I was going to say," I laugh.

When we get back to the reception, I see Dad has Lee on the dance floor. I walk over to Mom and hold my hand out to her.

She takes my hand and gracefully rises to her feet. When we get to the dance floor, I look down at her, thinking she's getting shorter.

"Are you shrinking?" I ask as we begin to dance.

"Lake, you're never too old for a smack upside the head," she warns, then a smile stretches over her face, "I'm only wearing three-inch heels today."

I let out a chuckle and hold her a little tighter.

She shifts her hand from my arm to my cheek. "No matter how old you are, and whether you have children of your own, you'll always be my beautiful baby boy."

Coming to a standstill, I let go of her hand and wrap both my arms around her.

"It fills me with so much pride to be your son," I whisper. "I love you, Mom."

"Thank God I'm wearing waterproof mascara," she sniffles against my chest.

Dad and Lee stop next to us. "Let's switch. I want to dance with my sexy wife."

"Yeah, you're traumatizing me right now," I grumble as I let go of Mom and take Lee's hand.

Dad wags his eyebrows at mom. "Hey baby, do you want to go home with me tonight."

"Todd, do you want to walk out of here tonight on your own two legs?" Mom scolds him. "Try calling me baby again."

As the song ends and there's a moment's silence, Kingsley's phone begins to ring.

'It's your daddy calling, and you know he's gonna chew your ear off.'

"Oh crap," she hisses while digging for her phone.

'It's your daddy calling, all you're gonna hear is blah, blah, blah, blah, blah.'

I let out a burst of laughter when she tips her whole bag over on the table, and all I see is candy scattering everywhere.

She finally finds it and answers sweetly, "Hi, Daddy."

"Never a dull moment," I murmur as I turn my attention back to Lee. "Come here." I pull her to my chest, and we just sway to the music.

Chapter 22

Lake

On the drive over to the hotel, I notice Lee growing quieter until she's just silently staring straight ahead.

Before she stops breathing, I say, "Relax, nothing's going to happen tonight."

Her head snaps to me. "Why?"

"I don't want you to feel pressured. Just because we're married doesn't mean we have to have sex immediately. We'll let it happen naturally."

"Okay," she whispers, looking a little more relaxed.

Knowing she's reserved, has me wondering whether she might have any questions she's not asking out of fear of being embarrassed.

"And now that we're married," I begin to say, trying to find words that won't make this awkward for her, "you know you can ask or tell me anything, right?"

She nods, smiling at me before she returns her gaze to the road.

"So, you don't have any questions about being intimate?" I try again.

This time she doesn't look at me, but instead, she brings her one hand up to her cheek, pressing her fingers against her blushing skin. "It's too embarrassing," she whispers.

I reach a hand over to her hands, which are resting on her lap, and I give them a squeeze before I return mine to the steering wheel. "It's okay. I don't want you to feel uncomfortable."

After a little while, she whispers, "Will it hurt?"

I have done so much research on that subject, which I'm thankful for right now. "It's different for everyone. If..." Shit, how do I say this? "If your body... is well prepared, it shouldn't hurt. There might be some initial discomfort."

"Really?" she asks, a hopeful look on her face as she glances at me.

I reach over for her hand again. "Really." And because I don't want to discuss the subject in the heat of the moment, I ask, "Are you on any form of contraceptive?"

She shakes her head.

"In that case, I'll wear protection."

"Why?" she asks, with a look of confusion on her face. "How will I conceive so I can bear an heir then?"

"We can wait until we're older. We're not in a rush... are we?"

"We aren't? Won't your parents be upset?"

"No. They were married eight years before they had me."

A wide smile spreads over her face, and she completely relaxes next to me.

"Is that what you've been worried about? That I'd expect you to fall pregnant right away?"

When she nods, I'm honestly surprised, and then she explains, "I thought that's why the marriage was arranged, so I could provide a child."

"It's settled then. I'll wear protection until we both agree we're ready to have children. I'll also make an appointment for you with a doctor so you can start with the pill."

"Okay." She leans her head back and just watches me with a smile around her mouth.

I'm so glad we had this talk. It makes me feel better knowing we're on the same page moving forward.

When we arrive at the hotel, I check us in. Once we walk into the presidential suite, I begin to feel the effects from the day's excitement.

Lee closes the door while I go place our bags in the bedroom.

Coming back into the living room, I see Lee glancing out the window. I walk up behind her and wrap my arms around her, resting my chin on her head.

She brushes a fingertip over my wedding band, and says, "Thank you for the beautiful rings you had made."

"You're welcome."

She pulls her ring off and takes a closer look at the gemstone.

"It's Alexandrite. I chose the stone because it's rare, just like our love." She turns around in my arms, so she's facing me.

Then she lifts the ring closer to her face, and I watch her lips part when she sees the inscription. "In this life, the next, and thereafter." When she looks up at me, there's so much happiness on her face, and it resonates inside me. "It's perfect."

She puts the ring on again, and then I bend down and placing a hand under her knees, I pick her up. "I'm carrying my wife to bed on our wedding night," I tease.

Walking into the bedroom, I set her down on the bed, then press a kiss to her mouth. "You get ready first."

"I'll be quick." She grabs her bag and darts into the bathroom while I go switch off the light in the living room.

I check my phone for any messages, while Lee finishes in the bathroom. When she comes out, wearing a bathrobe, I grab my t-shirt and sweatpants, and as I walk by her, I quickly press a kiss to her lips.

I shower and go through my routine, thinking how awesome it's going to be now that I get to fall asleep with her in my arms every night.

When I'm done, and I open the door, I see Lee sitting on the side of the bed with a slight smile on her face, looking deep in thought.

She glances up when I get close to her, and instantly her smile widens, and it makes my heart expand with love for her.

"You must be tired after today. Let's get some sleep," I say.

She stands up and bringing her hands to my face, she pulls me down so she can press a kiss to my mouth. Thinking it's a goodnight kiss, I begin to pull back, but then she stretches up on her toes, and her lips part against mine.

I take a step closer and wrap my arm around her waist, tilting my head to the side.

Brushing her tongue over mine, Lee deepens the kiss, and it takes only seconds for heat to rush through my veins.

Her hands slip down my neck and chest, and when she takes hold of my shirt, and she begins to lift it, I break the kiss and search her face to make sure this is what she wants.

Seeing the love shining in her eyes steals my breath, and I help her pull the shirt over my head.

I watch as she lowers her eyes to my chest, and then she moves her hand closer, and her fingertips brush over my left shoulder and down to my abs. She traces the hard lines, and her smile softens with adoration.

I lift my hands to her neck and leaning down, I kiss her tenderly. When her fingers glide over my side, and she takes hold of the sweatpants, I begin to kiss her with more urgency.

Damn, where did I put the condoms?

I pull back so suddenly, Lee loses her balance and stumbling backward, she sits down on the bed.

"Sorry," I chuckle. "I just need to check something quickly." I dart to my bag, and luckily I find them in the first pocket I look in. I walk to the nightstand and set them down before I turn back to Lee, and placing my hands on either side of her on the bed, I lean over her, fusing our mouths together again.

When she begins to rise, I move an arm around her and pull her the rest of the way, as I straighten up. Our tongues taste and explore each other until we're gasping for air.

I raise my other hand to her neck and feel the softness of her skin as I trail it down. I begin to push the fabric back, and when it exposes her bare shoulder, I break the kiss and glance down. "You're not wearing anything under the robe?"

With the shake of her head, she reaches for the fabric, and my heartbeat speeds up a hell of a lot when she pulls the bathrobe open.

The sight of her naked body stuns me into a moment of pure awe. Slowly I reach for the fabric, and I push it off, wanting to see all of her. As the bathrobe pools at her feet, I brush my hand down from her shoulder until my fingertips graze the hardening bud of her breast.

There's so much wonder building in my chest as I let my hand curve around her breast, and brushing my thumb over her nipple, I feel it harden even more from my touch.

Moving my other hand behind her neck, I step closer until I feel her breasts press against my skin, and I glide my hand from her breast, down her side, and reaching the curve of her hip, my breath explodes over my lips as it speeds up from the exhilaration building inside of me.

My fingertips begin to tingle with anticipation, and it spreads through my body like a wildfire as I trail them down between her legs. Her lips part, and her breath hitches when the pad of my middle finger lightly makes contact with her clit.

Lee's cheeks flush, and goosebumps spread out over her skin, and I'm captivated by her reaction to my touch.

Slowly, I guide my finger to her opening, and as I start to push inside of her, she tilts her face up to mine. Her eyes shine with emotion as she silently expresses the significance of this moment to me.

I'm the first man to touch her, and knowing it fills me with so much gratitude.

This incredible woman belongs only to me.

Chapter 23

Lee

The way Lake looks at me… I see the colors of a hundred sunrises in his eyes – a promise of the years to come.

His touch makes me feel cherished, and it fills me with the reassurance that I'm the most important person to him.

Lake loves me.

Tears born from his pure and profound love for me fill my eyes.

As he pushes his finger inside me, my breath catches in my throat from the immense wave of sensations the touch sends through my body. It feels like I'm standing at a threshold, and one more touch from Lake will give birth to a new me – my days of being a girl behind me, and the years of being a woman ahead of me.

Lake pulls his hand away from between my legs and lifting me up against him, he takes a step forward, and then he carefully lays me down in the middle of the bed.

I'm able to see the power rippling beneath his skin as he moves, and it makes me feel so unbelievably safe.

Lake's eyes meet mine, and a smile slowly forms around his mouth as he moves his hand back to between my legs. Cupping me, he pushes his finger back inside me, going deeper as his palm presses down on me.

My heartbeat speeds up while my eyes blink slower, and it feels like a spell is being cast over me, numbing all my other senses and heightening every sensation of Lake's touch.

He pulls his hand away again, and moves it over my abdomen and up to my breasts, tenderly caressing my body.

Lowering his head closer to mine, his hand keeps rubbing over my skin, and when he begins to caress me with a firmer touch, he crushes his mouth to mine.

Waves of tingles crash over me and unable to keep still, I bring my hands to his jaw. I turn my body into his, feeling an overwhelming need to be closer to him.

It feels as if Lake's tongue is dancing with mine, and this time when he moves his hand down, and he pushes a finger inside of me, he begins to knead me in a way that makes sensations spin in my abdomen, creating a whirlwind of pleasure.

My breaths race into his mouth, and soon I'm left gasping. I can feel a moan build up in my chest as the whirlwind grows within me, and when the sound escapes over my lips, the wind blows through every part of my body, robbing me of my breath.

I didn't even realize I shut my eyes, and opening them, I see Lake's gaze locked on my face in stunned awe. Whispering, he asks, "How's it possible that you become more beautiful every time I blink? Are you even human?"

Too breathless, and still trembling from pleasure, I can only nod.

His eyes start to shine. "Do you have any idea how much I love you?"

"Yes," I whisper, and when I've managed to catch my breath, I continue, "It's the same unconditional love I have for you. It's so strong and endless; it will last me a thousand lifetimes."

286

Lake pulls away from me, and when he steps out of his sweatpants, and I see him naked for the first time, there's no sign of the embarrassment I thought I'd feel.

I drink in the sight of my husband, and when he's finished rolling on the condom, and he places a knee on the bed so he can crawl over me, I reach for him.

As soon as he lowers himself to me, I wrap my arms around him. My hands brush over the broad expanse of his back, and I revel in the feel of his muscles rippling under his skin as he positions himself between my legs.

When I feel him pressing against my opening, I glance down, and the love I feel for Lake grows into something sacred as I watch him push inside of me.

When I only feel pressure and slight discomfort, my body relaxes, allowing me to focus on how it feels to become one with Lake.

When he's fully sheathed in me, he rests his arms on either side of my head, and his eyes find mine. His hips begin to draw back, and his lips part as a breath rushes over them. Pushing into me again, his face fills with so much emotion, it escapes from his eyes and bathes me in wonderment.

We're held captive by each other as we consummate our love. I feel him move inside of me, and knowing it will only ever be him fills me with unspeakable joy.

Lake moves his arm down between us, and his mouth finds mine as he begins to rub the bundle of nerves above my opening. His tongue strokes mine, and his thrusts speed up, each one growing with intensity as the whirlwind of sensations returns to wreak havoc inside of me.

A desperate moan rushes from me, and it only makes Lake kiss me with an urgency that makes my body writhe against his.

His breath catches, and he breaks the kiss. Locking his gaze with mine, he increases the pressure on my bundle of nerves, and my body begins to jerk beneath his with each flash of light brought on by the intense pleasure streaking through me, and it illuminates everything that I am to Lake.

His features tighten with so much emotion, it brings tears to my eyes, and as he begins to shudder against me, a tear escapes and rolls over my temple. Seeing Lake above me, I know with absolute certainty, I will never see anything as beautiful as my husband while he empties himself inside of me.

Lake brings his arm back up and rests it beside my head. He lowers his head until I feel his breaths rushing over my shoulder.

We lie still for a little while, and when our breathing starts to return to normal, he lifts his head. My gaze finds his, and when I see the tears in his eyes, another escapes from mine.

"I didn't expect it to be so intense," he whispers, his voice hoarse from everything we felt and shared.

"Thank you," the words rush from me as more tears flood my eyes. "Thank you for choosing me to be your wife."

I wish I had the words to tell him how blessed I feel, but instead, I can only show him my tears, each one filled with more happiness than most people will ever get to experience in their entire lives.

Lake

Waking, I open my eyes, and a smile curves the corner of my mouth when I see Lee staring back at me.

"How long have you been awake?" I ask, and reaching for her, I pull her body close to mine.

"I don't know. I got lost in time while watching you sleep," she whispers. She snuggles against me, and I bury my face in her hair as I hold her tighter.

"Hmm… can we stay in bed all day?" I murmur, feeling so satisfied with my life right now, I just want to bask in it for a couple of hours.

"We could, but –" my stomach growls, and she lets out a chuckle, "I don't think you'll last long without food." Pulling back, she presses a kiss to my chin. "You can stay in bed while I go get us food."

I shake my head. "No, I don't mind starving if I get to hold you."

She pulls away from me and sits up.

Turning onto my back, I reach out to her and trail my fingers down her spine. Just touching her skin is enough to light a fire in me.

"How do you feel?" I ask, first wanting to hear if she's tender after last night before I take things further.

"Happy," she says, and it has me chuckling.

"I meant physically," I explain.

"Oh." She thinks about it for a moment, then she says, "I feel okay."

"Well, in that case." I grab hold of her and drag her back down to the mattress.

She lets out a shriek of laughter, and as I move over her, she opens her legs and then stills beneath me.

Her eyes sparkle as if fireflies have been captured in them, and when I grind my pelvis against hers, I watch them take flight.

Chapter 24

Lake

When I've gathered the last of my personal belongings in a box, I carry it out of the room, and seeing Mason and Falcon sitting on the couch, I set it down by the front door before I go to join them.

I raise my feet and rest them on the table, and leaning back against the couch, I stare at them.

"I'm not going to lie," Falcon says. "It hurts more than I thought it would."

"Yeah," Mason agrees.

"I'm downstairs," I say, even though I feel the same as them.

Half of me can't wait to get back to Lee. The other half... I close my eyes and lower my chin to my chest. "It hurts."

"For something new to start something has to end," Mason murmurs.

"Wow, look at you getting all deep," Falcon teases him.

The corner of Mason's mouth curves into a sad smile. "Guess I'm finally growing up." He leans his head back against the couch and lets out a sigh. "I'm scared."

Falcon and I keep quiet and wait for him to tell us why.

"What if I make a fucking mess of everything our grandfathers and fathers built? What if I ruin Kingsley's life by selfishly dragging her into mine? What if one of you needs me, and I'm too absorbed in making a profit... and I lose you?"

"You won't," Falcon says with certainty.

Mason looks at Falcon. "How do you know?"

"I know because you have never turned your back on Lake and me," Falcon meets Mason's eyes, "and we will never turn our backs on you. Before shit happens, we'll be there to help with CRC."

"As for Kingsley," I say. "Don't forget how strong she is. She will slap you upside the head if you start to derail. Money doesn't have the power to change everyone, Mason. I know for a fact Kingsley won't get absorbed in wealth, or power, or status, and deep down you know it too."

Mason nods, and a relieved smile spreads over his face.

I clear my throat before I say, "Lee and I have been talking."

Both Falcon and Mason's eyes snap to mine, and I hate the looks of apprehension that flash over their faces.

Focusing on Falcon, I ask, "If it's okay with you and Layla, we'd like to come along for the trip to Africa."

Surprise widens Falcon's eyes for a moment, and then he grins at me. "Is that a trick question?"

Then I look at Mason. "When we come back from Africa, we're going to look for a place close to you. We're still going to travel, but we want a home base to come back to."

"You're not fucking with me, right?" Mason asks, and his features tighten with emotion.

We all sit in silence for a little while, regaining control over our feelings.

"How will I be happy if I have to exchange one love for another?" I take a couple of deep breaths. "I can't choose between my brothers and my wife, and she doesn't expect me to."

Mason covers his mouth and wipes a tear away with a knuckle. I look to Falcon, and the relieved look on his face has me standing up. I walk around the table and squash myself in between them.

Falcon places his arm around my shoulders. "You have no idea how happy I am to hear that."

"Makes two of us," Mason mutters as he nudges me with his shoulder.

"Makes three of us," I add while sending up a prayer that I'll never have to make a choice like that.

After a while of getting swept up in our thoughts, Falcon says, "When we're in our forties, there's a good chance our kids will be living in this suite."

"Fuck," Mason grumbles.

"If I have a daughter, I'm moving in with her, "I say, which has Falcon and Mason chuckling. "I need to learn how to fire a shotgun."

"Now, there's a hobby the three of us can take up," Falcon agrees.

While we're preparing for our final exams, I go up to Falcon and Mason's suite while I study.

My mom has been picking Lee up every other day and showing her around so Lee can get acquainted with where all the different stores are for when we get our own place. Even Dad came by on Saturday to take Lee for a driving lesson.

I'm glad they're getting to know each other better, and it makes me feel less guilty about spending so little time with her.

"Damn, I hate law," I mutter as I stare at my laptop.

"I can't see shit. Where's the eye drops?" Falcon asks.

"Over there." Without looking away from his screen, Mason points toward the dining table where Layla left a study kit she made for us.

It's funny how slowly time goes by when you have to do something boring.

Mason's phone starts ringing, and still keeping his eyes on the screen, he pats the cushion next to him until he finally finds his phone and answers with a grumble, "Chargill."

Suddenly the laptop gets shoved to the side, and Mason jumps up. "Are you sure?"

When relief swipes his feet from under him, and he sits back down, I move my laptop to the side. "Falcon," I call, while I lean forward, waiting for Mason to finish the call.

"Thank you so much," Mason says. "Thanks for letting me know." He listens and then responds, "You have a good day as well."

Falcon comes out of the room, blinking from putting in eyedrops.

Mason sets his phone down on the table and says, "That was the DA. They charged Serena with assault and placed her under house arrest."

"Awesome," Falcon says as he sits down. "That alone has to be hell for her."

"They're going to try and get a two-year community service sentence."

"Oh, she's going to love that," I chuckle. "I'd pay to see her waist-deep in a dumpster while she has to clean it."

"I just feel relieved that she'll receive some sort of punishment. It would've sucked if she found a way to buy herself out of the case going to court," Falcon adds.

"The court case itself will go on for a while, and she'll be stuck at home for the duration. So that's an added bonus," I comment.

"Yes, shit," Mason darts up and rushes to the door. "I'm going to tell Kingsley."

When he's out the door, I look to Falcon, who's still blinking.

"How many drops did you put in?" I ask, and getting up, I walk to his bathroom and wet a facecloth under cold water. When I get back to him, I say, "Lean your head back and close your eyes."

"Yes, Dad," Falcon grumbles.

I wipe gently over his eyes, and then he smiles. "That's nice. Just keep doing it for a while."

"You can be glad I love you," I mumble under my breath.

Lee

(Two months later...)

"We're all going," Mom says, wiggling her eyebrows at Lake.

I'm still trying to get used to calling Lake's parents Mom and Dad, but it's getting easier every time I see them.

"Just the two of you, or everyone?" Lake asks.

"The entire CRC clan," Dad answers. "Even Julian is coming. Warren didn't give him a choice." He lets out a chuckle. "Since the divorce proceedings started and the DA charged Clare, Warren can finally get on with his life."

I feel sorry for Mr. Reyes, Julian, and Falcon that Clare turned out to be such a monstrous person.

"Where in Africa are we going to?" I ask. Last I spoke to Layla she was waiting to hear where her father will be situated once summer vacation started.

"Warren spoke with Layla's father, and it seems we're all heading to Namibia," Dad answers.

"Cool," Lake says, "Where in Africa is that?"

Mom lets out a chuckle. "South-West coast."

Once dinner is over, we walk out of the restaurant with Lake's parents, and I hug Mom before we go our separate ways.

"I think I ate too much," Lake complains as he rubs over his stomach.

Glancing at him with a mischievous grin, I tease, "I know of a way you can work all the food off."

"Is that so?" He reaches for my hand, but laughing, I dart away.

"We first have to meet the real estate agent before we can go back to the dorm," I remind him.

"I can always reschedule the appointment for another time," Lake says, and shooting forward, he grabs hold of my arm and pulls me toward him. He wraps his arm around my waist and presses a kiss to my mouth. "Right now, I think an entire night of exercise will be needed to work off everything I ate."

"I guess it's a good thing I had a nap this afternoon."

Standing under a lamppost, Lake smiles down at me, "Are you looking forward to your first family vacation?"

Grinning up at him, I nod. "I think it's going to be an amazing experience for everyone to be together."

"And after we get back, we can decorate our new home," he says as we begin to walk toward the car.

I glance up at the stars that shine over the country I've now accepted as my own and thinking back on the past four months, I can't believe how much my life has changed.

"Salanghaeyo," I whisper to Lake as I press my cheek to his arm.

"Salanghaeyo," he says as we get to the car, and turning to face me, he leans down and presses a tender kiss to my mouth. Pulling back, he whispers, "Just look at my beautiful wife. How lucky am I?"

Epilogue

Falcon

By the time we get to Shipwreck Lodge, our home for the next two weeks, we're all tired and hungry.

Dad booked the entire place with the help of Stephanie and Mr. Shepard, of course.

The off-road vehicle which our tour guide, Theo, calls a Jeep comes to a stop at the lodge. There are shipwreck-shaped chalets scattered across the sand, and in the middle is a restaurant.

As we all climb off the vehicles, we form a group.

"Welcome to Skeleton Coast National Park, my friends," Theo says loudly so we can hear him above the wind. "I'm going to let you settle into your chalets. At sundown, we can drive out to an oasis for a magical hour before returning for dinner." The African man speaks with so much enthusiasm it's contagious, and I feel the bite of excitement return after the long drive.

Staff members of the lodge come to help offload our luggage from the Jeeps, and once we've all been allocated a chalet, we trudge through the desert sand.

"The first cabin is mine," Dad calls out.

"We know, Dad," I yell back at him. "And it's called a chalet!"

"Whatever!" he shouts, and then I see him chuckle.

I take Layla's hand and help her through the sand, and glancing at Lake and Lee, I smile as he picks her up and carries her to their chalet.

"Look," Layla points to Mason, who has Kingsley tossed over his shoulder.

I let out a sigh. "Some things will never change."

The chalet is definitely not five-star, but then five-star accommodations would ruin the experience.

Once we've satisfied our curiosity inside, Layla and I go to ask Dad and Stephanie if they want to join us for a walk.

"What do you mean a walk," Dad grumbles as he steps off the porch. "We'll be climbing dunes while we're here."

"Let's go climb a dune, Warren," Stephanie says wryly, and she starts walking, not giving him much of a choice.

As we head toward the first dune, I glance at Layla and noticing she's chewing on her thumbnail, I pull her hand away from her mouth. "Are you anxious to see your Dad?"

She nods. "I can't wait. I don't want to walk too far in case he comes while we're gone."

"We'll just see what's on the other side of this dune," I say to put her at ease.

"Hold up!" Mason hollers and glancing over my shoulder I see the Chargills and Cutlers making their way toward us.

"Kiddo!" Layla's head whips in the direction of her mother, who's pointing at something, and when she sees a man walking toward us, she begins to cry as she breaks out in a run.

Or at least she tries to, but the sand keeps slowing her down.

"Daddy!" she screams and hearing the happiness in her voice makes me feel so damn emotional, I have to hold myself back so she can have this moment with her father.

"Aww... I'm going to cry," Kingsley says behind me.

Layla practically throws herself at her father, and they both tumble down on the side of a dune. The wind catches their laughter and carries it over the desert.

"Let's go, slowpoke," Mr. Chargill says to Mason as he heads toward my dad.

An arm falls around my shoulder and glancing to my side, I see Julian grinning. "I haven't seen him this happy in all my life."

I follow his line of sight to where Dad is standing on top of the dune. "I'm king of the world," he shouts and almost loses his balance, but luckily Stephanie is there to grab hold of his arm.

"Honestly, Warren. You're not yesterday's child anymore," she chastises him.

"What are you talking about. I'm in my prime," he argues.

Layla and her father head back in our direction, and I gesture toward them. "Let's go meet my future father-in-law."

As I approach them, Layla excitedly tugs on her father's arm. "Daddy, this is my Falcon."

The way she introduces me brings a huge smile to my face and eases some of the nervousness that's been building.

I reach a hand out to Mr. Shepard, who looks like he could be a park ranger in his safari gear.

"It's a pleasure to finally meet you, Sir. Layla has told me so much about you."

He takes my hand, and after shaking, he doesn't let go. He stares at me for a good minute, but I don't drop my eyes from his.

"Now I understand," he finally murmurs.

"Sir?"

"I understand why my daughter loves you." He tugs me closer, and then he hugs me, which has me giving Layla a what-the-hell-is-happening-look over his shoulder.

She just smiles at us.

Mr. Shepard pats me hard on the back, and when he lets go, he says, "Words can be deceiving, but a man's eyes never lie.

"John," Stephanie calls out, and when he looks her way, she waves.

"Let me go greet the rest of the people," he excuses himself.

I tilt my head and look at Layla. "That went okay, right?"

"He approves of you," she shrieks, a wide smile on her face.

"I'd say it went well," Julian says from next to me.

As we stop at the beach and climb off the Jeeps, I don't know who's more at awe of the sight before us.

"U-wa," Lee murmurs from next to Lake, and I smile because I love when she gets so swept up at the moment that she switches over to Hangul.

"Welcome to the place God made in anger," Theo roars with his African accent, and it just lends to the amazement of it all. "Portuguese sailors also called it the gates of hell."

For as far as the eye can see, the Atlantic ocean rushes to shore, clashing with the oldest desert on the planet.

We all stand in silence for a long while, and when our tour guide walks up the stretch of beach, he begins to hum a tribal tune that is swept up by the wind, and it makes it sound like… Africa.

I go to stand next to Dad.

"I've accomplished so many great things in my life," he whispers. "But standing here, I feel humbled. I've missed the feeling."

I place my hand on his back, and as my gaze drifts over the CRC family, both old and new, I feel unbelievably thankful.

Layla comes to stand on Dad's other side, and I take a couple of steps backward. She hooks her arm through Dad's and lays her cheek against his arm, and then she whispers, "Thank you."

Dad shakes his head. "I'm the one who's thankful. You've given me one of the greatest gifts I've ever received." She glances up at him, and when their eyes meet, he whispers, "An experience."

Thank you for taking this incredible journey

with me.

That was my original message, but as I type the final words to what I can only describe as an awe-inspiring experience, I'm filled with such joy.

These characters, I can't let go of them yet, and that's why I'm writing an extended version of the Epilogue.

There's still Julian, and of course, the next generation of Trinity Academy & The Enemies To Lovers Series.

I'll keep you all up to date on my social media pages.

Love, Michelle x

Trinity Academy

FALCON

Novel #1

Falcon Reyes & Layla Shepard

MASON

Novel #2

Mason Chargill & Kingsley Hunt

LAKE

Novel #3

Lake Cutler & Lee-ann Park

THE EPILOGUE

Novel #4

JULIAN

Novel #5

A Stand Alone Novel

Julian Reyes & Jamie Truman

Enemies To Lovers

The Next Generation

COMING 2020

HUNTER
Novel #1
Hunter Chargill (*Mason and Kingsley's son*)
&
Jade Daniels (*Rhett & Evie's daughter*)

KAO
Novel #2
Kao Reed (*Marcus and Willow's son*)
&
Fallon Reyes (*Falcon & Layla's daughter*)

NOAH
Novel #3
Noah West (*Jaxson & Leigh's son*)
&
Carla Reyes (*Julian & Jamie's daughter*)

RIKER
Novel #4
Ryker West (*Logan & Mia's son*)
&
Danny Hayes (*Carter & Della's daughter*)

CHRISTOPHER
Novel #5
Christopher Hayes – (*Carter & Della's son*)
&
Dash West – (*Jaxson & Leigh's daughter*)

FOREST
Novel #6
Forest Hayes (*Carter & Della's son*)
&
Aria Chargill (*Mason & Kingsley's daughter*)

TRISTAN
Novel #7
Tristan Hayes – (*Carter & Della's son*)
&
Hana Cutler – (*Lake & Lee's daughter*)

JASE
Novel #8
Jase – (*Julian & Jamie's son*)
&
Mila – (*Logan & Mia's Daughter*)

Connect with me

Newsletter

FaceBook

Amazon

GoodReads

BookBub

Instagram

Twitter

Website

About the author

Michelle Heard is a Bestselling Romance Author who loves creating stories her readers can get lost in. She loves an alpha hero who is not afraid to fight for his woman.

Want to be up to date with what's happening in Michelle's world? Sign up to receive the latest news on her alpha hero releases → NEWSLETTER

If you enjoyed this book or any book, please consider leaving a review. It's appreciated by authors.

Acknowledgments

Sheldon, you're my everything. Thank you for staying by my side. I must've done something right in a previous life to be blessed with such an amazing gift as you in this life. Happy 21st! Love, Mom.

To my beta readers, Kelly, Elaine, Sarah, and Leeann – Thank you for being the godparents of my paper-baby.

Sherrie, Sheena, and Allyson – Thank you for listening to me ramble, for reading and rereading the Trinity Academy series with me.

Candi Kane PR - Girl, thank you for being patient with me and my bad habit of missing deadlines.

Wander & David – Thank you for giving Lake the perfect look.

A special thank you to every blogger and reader who took the time to take part in the cover reveal and release day.

Love ya all tons ;)